STORY HARVEST

Fresh-Picked Tales

Scribes Valley Publishing
Knoxville, Tennessee
scribesvalley.com

The stories in this anthology are works of fiction. Characters, names, places, and incidents are products of the authors' imagination or are used fictitiously.

ISBN: 978-1-7349744-1-6

Scribes Valley Publishing Company
Knoxville, Tennessee
www.scribesvalley.com

The publisher is not responsible for websites—or content on those websites—not owned by the publisher.

DEDICATION

This anthology is dedicated to those
who enjoy freshly-picked stories!

TO THE AUTHORS FEATURED IN THIS BOOK:

Scribes Valley Publishing sincerely thanks you
for your time, patience, trust, and talent.

CONTENTS

GROWING STORIES
A Foreword by David L. Repsher, editor

It starts with a spark. An idea that comes from nowhere, appearing suddenly and without warning, triggered by a sight, a sound, a feeling, an overheard conversation, or even nothing at all.

The author grabs that spark and plants it in the fertile "soil" of their brain. There they help it to grow as they pamper, shape, and mold it into a well-developed story.

Some stories mature rapidly, becoming fully grown almost immediately. Others take more time to develop as the author considers and reconsiders how the story should flow.

The finished story can be what the author intended from the beginning, or be completely different from the spark that started it all.

Such is the wonder and amazement of the story growing process. There are no limits to the author's imagination. A story can carry an idea straight through, or have pieces of the idea changed and re-changed until the author decides it is perfect. *A word of warning*: the author may feel the story will *never* achieve perfection. This is normal as the author believes there is always room for improvement. But the author *will* eventually reach a point where they are willing to share the story with readers.

And then the harvest begins!

Read on to discover the freshly picked fruits of this story harvest. We at Scribes Valley think you will agree that the featured authors grew their stories just right!

FIRST PLACE

TANGERINE STRANDS

The little girl and boy were screaming.

Not the bad screaming.

Not *Mia's* screaming.

Lucretia stood in the outer schoolyard, looking through the fence that separated her from the scene of the crime she had created two months prior. Of all the kids packed into the limited pen designated for kindergarten students, her eyes and ears couldn't help but track the running, laughing—*For now*, she thought—screaming little girl and boy, engaged in the age-old interplay: the fluttering of the little girl's long hair; the little boy's outstretched hand; the former barely outrunning the latter, whether by choice or biology, laughing, screaming, most times out of exhilaration, sometimes because a primitive thought told her she was in genuine danger; the way the invisibly tethered pair navigated the other children, who were merely sitting ducks oblivious to the fast-paced game of tandem sparrows; the little boy finding a latent gear, accelerating, reaching with a clawed hand, closer, closer, closer; the little girl abruptly turning to avoid his fingers; the chase slowing down—*this* time—to recover for an encore, or dying altogether, the dangerous game saved for something as distant as another day, or as close as the next recess.

And outside of this customary exchange, outside of this playground within a playground, Lucretia felt relief, for the little girl and boy had yet again successfully avoided recreating the history that had taken place in there.

She and Mia's history.

A history she had forgotten until last week.

Lucretia had looked forward to the first day of school. Her mother had dropped her off at the side of the building, wished her good luck on her first day of school, and drove away to the job that paid their rent. Mia's mother, on the other hand...well, if she had work, she had clearly called in sick so as to protect her daughter from Lucretia.

It was in the gymnasium, where the buzzing student body waited to be assigned their new teachers, that Lucretia had felt the summer's sunburns in her gut, the summer's scraped knees all over her body, for she had seen for the first time how and in what condition Mia had spent *her* summer—thanks to that single moment in June.

Thanks to Lucretia.

The little girl and boy were screaming again.

Not the bad screaming.

Not *Mia's* screaming.

Not yet, Lucretia thought.

She looked away from the potential violence, and focussed on the one obstacle she would need to overcome if now was indeed the time to do what she hadn't any real courage to do. But when the obsidian eyes of Ms. Jackson, perched atop the steps leading to Lucretia's assigned door, met hers, she panicked, resorting to blindly surveying the vast schoolyard available to her.

She knew her new world by heart: the field that was home to two continental versions of football, haloed by quintuplet tracks; faded baseball diamond; fully-loaded play area—just some of the perks of becoming a full-day student in the first grade.

The perks, however, did nothing to perk her up.

Everyone was out here, relishing their twenty minutes outside the stifling classrooms, trying to capture as much of the lingering dog days as possible. Everyone who stole glances of Mia, who never saw, but must have felt the judging eyes. Everyone who gossiped, but pretended otherwise, as if the school was ripe with other Mias.

Everyone was out here.

Except Mia.

Lucretia could bear the Mia-less vista no longer. Heavy guilt shepherded her heavy legs toward Ms. Jackson. She could have claimed to have felt ill—she was, after all, sick with nerves—but opted for a watered-down lie that the hateful teacher would likely deny. "Can I get a drink, Ms. Jackson?" Her voice cracked, supporting her cause.

Ms. Jackson smiled, opened the door, and held it for the stunned Lucretia. She eyed the teacher as she crossed the threshold. The woman indeed appeared to be the same Ms. Jackson who had cradled and cooed the wailing Mia on that day in June; the same Ms. Jackson who glared and yelled at the culpable Lucretia. *Doesn't she remember me?* Lucretia mused. *Doesn't she remember what I did?*

The hard handrail felt like a slippery serpent of electric nerves. With legs of quicksand, she began the long ascent. She caught up to her pounding heart upon reaching the second-floor landing. There, the pair of heavy doors guarded against her, protecting whom she sought. But they were no match for a mousy thumb pressing the latch.

The click of the stairwell door did nothing to interrupt the hushed voices wafting over to her from the opposite side of the hallway. While the volume of the conversation rose with every step toward the only open door, specific words refused to clarify themselves. Still, Lucretia discerned two voices: one she knew, but scarcely heard during class; the other could have belonged to either relief or dread, for Mia's mother was prone to classroom visits between the usual drop-offs and pick-ups—which contributed to the list of gossip topics.

Please be Mrs. Atwood, she thought.

Lucretia reached the door, and listened for whether or not she would abort her mission. When her heart, thudding in her ears, skipped a beat, she heard not dread, but relief—*Mrs. Atwood!*— and turned the corner just as another thought occurred to her: *Mia's mother could still be in there, not talking.*

Two pairs of eyes looked up at her from their respective desks. One pair looked back down just as quickly. The other pair held her gaze. "Hey, Lucretia." There was a tinge of surprise in Mrs. Atwood's voice. Surprise turned to concern. "You okay?"

Lucretia knew she looked as dishevelled and antsy and nauseous as she felt. "Yeah," she croaked. "Just..." She couldn't lie about needing a drink; she had passed the fountains on her way over.

"Too hot outside?" Mrs. Atwood offered.

"Yeah," Lucretia exhaled, relieved for the out.

"Well, you can take your seat if you like. Recess is almost over, anyway. Speaking of..." Mrs. Atwood rose from her desk. "Girls, I'll be right back. Gotta use the ladies' room." She turned to the damaged thing at the far end of the second-last row, peeling a tangerine. "We'll talk some more about it later, okay, Mia?"

Lucretia wondered if Mrs. Atwood saw the pain, suffering, and sadness that animated Mia's barely nodding head. She wondered if Mrs. Atwood knew that *she* was responsible for those emotions. *Of course, she does,* Lucretia reminded herself. *Mia and her mother and Ms. Jackson for sure told her what I did.*

Mrs. Atwood flashed Lucretia a smile on her way out.

Victim and criminal were alone.

Lucretia remained at the door. Staring at Mia, like the other kids. Talking about her, like the other kids, except her conscience was the mouth, tongue-tied, inarticulate. Her meagre vocabulary boiled down to a single thought: *Just do it, chicken!*

Paring herself from the linoleum, Lucretia shuffled toward the row of desks in a wide arc, simultaneously avoiding and gravitating toward the back row. Her eyes never left Mia, who busied herself with her tangerine. As she drew reluctantly closer, Lucretia was afforded a profile view of the baseball cap—a *major* topic of gossip—that never left Mia's head. Having reached the beginning of the back row, she then trudged the never-ending trudge toward her ill-placed desk at the very end.

Each timid step brought her closer to Mia.

Each fearful step brought her closer to the damned baseball cap...and what it hid.

Each outright terrified step packed more and more of Mia's citrusy snack into her nose.

Standing behind her chair, which sat behind her desk, which sat behind Mia, Lucretia wondered why Mia's mother—who had witnessed the unfortunate seating plan during several of her visits—allowed the criminal so close to her daughter.

Lucretia heard Mia's chewing slow, saw her back stiffen, growing uncomfortably aware of Lucretia's presence, and the lack of chair legs scraping against the floor.

Chicken! Chicken! CHICKEN!

She collapsed, rather than sat in, her poorly-assigned seat, and couldn't help but fall into the week-long habit of studying the bit of naked scalp visible under the rim of Mia's baseball cap. She memorized the bony ridges, the shallow pockets, the pronounced point where the skull met the spine, the precise number of pink and red bumps. She knew each of Mia's five beauty-marks intimately, and no matter how many times her eyes played with them, she couldn't settle upon a shape, pattern, or design. She believed that if the school day were longer, she would finally be able to count each terribly short bristle of thin hair.

A fresh burst of tangerine invaded Lucretia's nose. The odour divided itself: southbound, to her stomach, where it mixed with and churned breakfast; northbound, to the mysterious region of the brain where scent converted to imagery. There, she saw that bright June day, not too dissimilar from the little girl and boy outside. *Did he catch her?* she wondered. *Is she crying?*

Chicken! that other part of her taunted.

What if she doesn't believe me?

Chicken!

What if she screams and cries again?
Chicken!
What if she hits me?
CHICKEN!

Another burst of tangerine perspiration. This time Lucretia didn't see the little girl and boy, but another film entirely: the claustrophobic kindergarten playground; Mia clutching the back of her head, bawling in Ms. Jackson's arms; Lucretia trying her best not to join in on the bawling, but failing, trying to give back the long brunette strands of hair wrapped around her stubby fingers; Mia blaring her refusal; Lucretia covering her blubbering face, her snotty nose detecting something flowery, something fruity.

Yet another surge of Mia's tangerine, and Lucretia realized that Mia's envied, rope-like hair had been washed in tangerine-scented shampoo that day in June.

"I'm sorry." Lucretia craved to be heard, perhaps even to be forgiven, and yet she didn't understand why Mia was turning to face her.

"For what?" Mia asked.

Lucretia couldn't believe the question more than the fact Mia was actually talking to her. *Did she forget, too? Like Ms. Jackson? Does her mom remember?*

Mia started to turn away.

The tangerine had completely assimilated with Lucretia's stomach contents, and out came a vomit of sorts: "I'm sorry for pulling your hair and for making you cry and for making all your hair fall out of your head and eyebrows and everyone talking about you and looking at you and not playing with you and making you not want to go outside and play..." As she purged, she saw the most peculiar thing: a smile. Mia had never looked so pretty. Lucretia thought Mia had been pretty on their last day as kindergartners, when she had asked if she'd like to play tag, but this was...

...beauty.

Lucretia sealed her spewing. She noted a sliver of pale orange flesh stuck between Mia's big teeth, somehow enhancing her beautiful smile.

"You didn't pull all my hair out, Luke," Mia said, her voice tickled by a suppressed laugh.

Lucretia—"Luke" to her only friend, Mia—saw two of the girl before her. Both Mia's lost their beautiful smiles as they took Lucretia's hand, and asked her why she was crying.

"I thought I..." Tears drowned the thought. "I thought I pulled out all your hair when we played tag that time."

"No," Mia said, beautiful smile nowhere on her lips. "I was sick."

"Sick? Like a cold?" Lucretia sniffled as if she bore the illness.

"I got leukemia," Mia said, the word somewhat shaky on her tongue.

Lucretia tasted the foreign word. "Lu-Luke-Mia?" She beamed. "Luke-Mia? Like our names?"

Mia smiled another one of her rainbows, tangerine pulp and all. "I never thought of that."

"What's Lu-Luke—"

"Leukemia," Mia corrected. "It's a bad sickness, but I don't got it anymore because the doctor gave me medicine, but the medicine makes your hair fall out. My mom is going to come to class one day soon, and help me and Mrs. Atwood tell everyone about it."

On the one hand, Lucretia was relieved to be off the hook. On the other, she now wished *she* had been the cause of Mia's hair loss. "Is that why you don't want to go outside?" The regret of the inquiry came as swiftly as Mia's radiant smile faded.

"I want to, but I can't do too much stuff, like running. I don't like the way the other kids look at me, and stuff." Now it was Lucretia's turn to wipe *her* duplicate self from Mia's brimming eyes.

The school bell rang, setting off an uproar outside.

Mrs. Atwood returned as if on cue. "You girls okay?" She hadn't noticed the swollen eyes. They smiled. "Mia, all good?" An extra smile from Mia.

Once again, Lucretia was gifted with the back of Mia's baseball-capped head, the way she would remain until the glancing and gossiping kids were summoned outside for more for-granted play. She leaned forward, and whispered each word louder than the next, for the rowdiness was racing up the steps. "If you want, I can play with you outside next recess." She saw the beauty-marks closest to each of Mia's ears rise ever so slightly, and she knew her friend was smiling.

And though the children were screaming in the hallway—not the bad kind of screaming; not *Mia's* screaming—Lucretia caught Mia's whisper: "Maybe we can play tag."

About the author:

An artisan baker by trade, Alfredo Salvatore Arcilesi has been published in over 50 literary journals worldwide. He was a finalist in the Blood Orange Review Literary Contest, and was awarded the Popular Vote in the Best of Rejected Manuscripts Competition. In addition to several short pieces, he is currently working on his debut novel.

SECOND PLACE

VISTA CRUISER
©2021 by William E. Burleson

I looked out the back window of our station wagon through twin plumes of swirling dust at our shrinking farmhouse on the hill. Betsy sat next to me in the back seat, driver's side. My sister paid no attention to anything outside the car, focusing instead on her two unclothed knock-off Barbie dolls as she played out some imagined same-sex waltz or argument or some other two-doll event. The dolls were new; Betsy had just had her seventh birthday the day before. I was ten. The four of us had a party—just the four of us—with the full treatment of cake and balloons and low-rent presents both of us knew to expect. I thought about saying something to her, maybe grabbing one of the dolls, maybe throwing it out the window. Our 1965 Vista Cruiser included the innovation of lap belts, but no one used them, making fights in the back seat epic. But that day, I was way too bored to even bother.

I laid the side of my head on one arm and looked at my dad driving and my mom next to him. Dad was so proud of that Oldsmobile Vista Cruiser. Sure, we had an old pickup, too. We were farmers, after all, growing corn and sometimes soybeans, and we had to have an old pickup. But that Vista Cruiser, now that was special. No one we knew had ever purchased a new car. Hell, I don't think we even knew anyone who knew someone who had bought a new car. Dad got it in blue, sporting the signature skylight windows on the top to better view all those mountains we would never go see. He bought it new three years before, paid for with the small life insurance policy his father carried. Grandpa intended it for a funeral in style, but the payout was worth enough for a pine box and a new Oldsmobile.

My parents sat quietly. Unusually so. Typically, a Saturday trip to town and the grocery store would include discussion of the logistics of life, the errands that needed to be run, the bills that needed to be paid. Not so that day. They simply looked forward, focused on the road.

The car slowed at the end of the dirt road, using the last of its momentum to crest the slope up to the highway. I looked up and down the state road—no cars, no nothing, except 180 degrees of blue sky, endless cornfields, and straight as an arrow blacktop.

My father looked left, and without coming to a complete stop, turned right, accelerating.

"Tom—"

"Don't start, Audrey. We'll be fine."

Now on clean, dry pavement, Dad cranked his window down, bringing a tornado into the back seat while barely ruffling his slick-black hair. To look at old pictures, he had been a handsome man, and it was easy to imagine what a young, pretty Audrey would have seen in him in his sharp army uniform. In the car that day, he wore a white T-shirt that stretched around his oversized shoulders and dirty work pants. My mom wore a flowered, spaghetti-strapped dress with a light-weight white sweater over her shoulders. I gave it no thought at the time, being a kid, but it must have made for a curious sight: my dirt-under-the-fingernails dad next to my perfectly dressed mother. A stranger might have asked: what event could both of these people be attending at the same time? Or, more accurately, considering we were miles from anything but other farms, where was my mom going as if dressed for a church dance? But she always dressed like that, and when at the grocery, she would wear makeup and heels while the other women would be in pants and work shirts. Needless to say, Mom would get a lot of sideways looks she never seemed to notice.

When Grandpa died, we inherited his farm. This was the farm Dad grew up on, the farm he left for Korea, leaving his older brother back to help and, presumably, take over the operation.

That's how it worked in farm country; the oldest got the farm. But in this case, a tractor tire fell on the uncle I never met, breaking his back, leaving him behind the barn for hours to die before Grandpa would wonder why he didn't come in for dinner. Now the farm belonged to Dad. He was happy to move back. Overjoyed, really. I understood years later that career-wise, things weren't going so well for him in the city. Going from one menial job to the next must have made going back to the farm a dream come true.

I looked at my mother looking out the window. There was nothing to look at out there but corn now six-foot high, but she seemed to be looking hard. I rolled down my window, wind smelling of pig shit increasing with each crank. My sister stayed at whatever game she was involved with by herself, except now her pigtails whipped around in the wind. My mop of red hair blew in all directions, and I liked the feeling of being in the center of a storm.

Dad reached down and came up with a cigarette. He fiddled with something and in a few seconds held the car lighter to his smoke, puffing once, twice, three times before reaching forward again to snap the lighter back where it belonged. He held the cigarette, resting his arm on the open window.

"Tom—"

"Audrey, your place is at home. You know that. Everybody knows that."

She turned to face her husband. "June is working at the Catholic school."

"That's their business."

I hated it when they argued, especially when I had no idea what it was about. When Mom yelled at Dad about getting drunk in town, even a ten-year-old understood that. When they argued about whether to travel to Grandma's in Chicago—got it. But I hated it when I felt like I walked in on an ongoing conversation where I missed the key facts explaining the strong feelings and hot collars.

"You're working all day," she said.

"Yes, exactly."

"Exactly what?"

"I'm working hard."

"My point is, you won't even notice. I'll leave your lunch out."

"And Jack and Betsy?"

My sister looked up, hearing her name, but just for a second.

"Jack's getting older."

If I hated hearing them talk about stuff I didn't understand, I doubly hated listening to them talk about me like I wasn't there.

Dad took a big drag on his cigarette, blowing the smoke forward, smoke swirling around before exiting the open windows. "You don't even know how to drive."

Mom had never learned how to drive. When that fact came out in conversations at the grocery or when visiting our school, it was met with a "Really?" every time. In the country, people had work to do, and how can you do it without being able to drive? She would say that she came from Chicago, and in Chicago, you have the El trains, so you don't need to drive. That answer didn't seem to satisfy anyone.

Mom and Dad met in Chicago after the war, a story they told regularly as if a totem for a happy family. He arrived in the Windy City on the way back to the plains, and he swept her off her feet; her family didn't approve, but she loved him, blah blah blah. They got married and got an apartment not far from Wrigley. Still, Mom's clan must have been able to see that he was a simple farmer with only one place to go.

"You can teach me, Tom," she said with an unrealistic breeziness as if trying to move the mood from one of contention to "let's do something fun together."

"Teach you?"

"Yeah. Don't you think it's time I learned?"

"You want to learn how to drive now."

"Yeah, I can help out that way."

He braked sharply, sliding me and my sister forward on the slippery seats, almost dumping us in the footwell. The Vista

Cruiser skidded to a stop on the gravel shoulder, dust kicking up all around. "Fine. I'll teach you." He got out and walked around the front of the car. Mom didn't move, as if not sure what was happening. He opened the passenger door and motioned with his cigarette, "Well, move over."

I couldn't see her expression, but she hesitated just a moment before sliding across the bench seat to behind the wheel. Dad got in the passenger side and closed the door.

"First, adjust the seat," he said, pointing down at something out of sight. They both rocked a bit until the seat lurched forward a couple inches. "Now the mirrors." He rolled down his passenger window as she carefully fussed with the mirror on the windshield before turning her attention to the driver's side.

"OK. Let's see how much you've been paying attention all these years." He flicked his cigarette out the window. "Three on a tree. You know where first is?"

"I think so."

"Well? What are you waiting for?"

She looked at him and at the shifter. "So, just pull it down?"

"Back and down."

I was fascinated and saw the opportunity to learn how to drive myself. I leaned on the seat, my head behind and between theirs, watching every move. Mom smiled, sitting up straight. One hand on the wheel, she took the shifter and wiggled it back and forth. It looked loose, flimsy, even. She pulled it down. The car made a terrible loud groaning noise.

"Not like that! Don't you know what a clutch is?"

"Clutch," she said in recognition of the failure, looking down to the pedals.

Dad leaned over, pointing. "Christ. Push it down and keep it down."

She did.

"Now shift it into first."

She pulled it back and down.

"OK, now slowly let out the clutch while applying the gas."

The car lurched and stalled.

"I said slowly!" He had her shift back into neutral and start the car, holding the starter on too long after the engine turned.

"Jesus, you are hopeless. Try again."

She did, stalling the car once more.

"Again."

This time, the car crept forward a few feet before stalling.

"Again."

My mother's thin, tan forearms were taut from gripping the wheel, knuckles porcelain. She stalled the car again, then again. "What am I doing wrong?" she said, looking down at the dashboard and pedals as if having forgotten some critical control.

"Do you mean with the car?"

She began to cry. All my life he would push her until she broke, and for what? None of it made any sense. I wanted to soothe her, make it all right, but I knew I couldn't. I had no idea how, and not for the first time I felt the frustration of uselessness.

"Again!"

She took a deep breath, looked up for a beat and then back down, and shifted it into gear. The car began to move down the shoulder.

"There you go," Dad said, probably more in a moment of pride in his teaching skills than in his wife's accomplishment. "Now check your mirror and steer onto the pavement."

Mom did as told, car weaving, correcting and overcorrecting, as the car picked up speed. She gunned it and let off, gunned it and let off, clearly unsure of the touch. She quickly smoothed it out, and the engine went from a baritone to a tenor.

"You need to shift. Let's do it this way: off the gas, clutch in."

She hesitated.

"Let off the gas, clutch in!"

She did and he reached over and shifted the lever back and up into second.

"Off the clutch, and give it the gas. That's it."

We picked up speed, engine winding up once again.

"Gas off, clutch in," he said. She did, and he pulled the lever down. "Give it the gas. There! Now you're driving."

I could only see Mom from the side, but she looked flushed and wet-faced but now with an excited smile. I looked at the speedometer, and we were going forty.

"Faster."

Mom gave it more juice, continuing to weave back and forth. Even my sister was paying attention now, eyes wide.

Dad reached out and put one hand on the wheel. "Easy now," he said, smoothing out the oversteering.

A truck approached. It zoomed by us, and my mom laughed.

"So now that you know how to drive, what are you going to do?"

She didn't say anything, as if not wanting to ruin the fun by returning to the original argument.

"Now maybe you can help out. But don't get it into your head that anything has changed. Clear?"

"Tom, nothing is going to change."

"Damn right. Who wears the pants?"

She sat quietly, now steering on her own, a little more competently every minute.

"Pants! Audrey, who wears the pants!?"

"You do, darling. You do."

"Yeah, goddam right."

I continued to lean on the seat ahead as we drove, now sixty. The wind blew around the car, and my sister rolled down her window, the last window, and she put both hands on the ledge looking out. Then,

"Tom—"

He punched the glove box. "What did I say? You mind your place, got it? I am not a failure! I am going to be fine!"

I leaned back, and Betsy and I looked at each other. She started to cry.

"It's 'we,' Tom."

"What?"

"'We' are going to be fine."

"No, I meant what I said. This is my farm and my life! You are no more useful than one more piece of livestock!"

Now it was all in, a full-on explosion. Been there before, and they always ended with broken plates and Dad drunk and no dinner and Mom apologizing and Betsy and I hiding in our rooms. But this time we had nowhere to flee.

Mom sobbed, rocking back and forth, hands still in a death grip on the wheel. "My sister warned me—"

"Don't talk about that bitch to me!"

"She warned me, everyone warned me!"

We went over a small hill fast enough for me to feel my stomach rise and fall. My sister cried and hugged her dolls to her chest. Mom sobbed, shaking her head as if to say no.

"You think so much of yourself. Big town girl. You are useless! I should have left when I knocked you up. Slut. But I did the stand-up thing, but do you care?"

Mom wailed even louder.

"Dad! No!" I heard myself yell. "Take it back!" I couldn't believe it, but it was clearly my voice.

He ignored me. "Count your blessings, Audrey, that's all I can say."

"Blessings? You call this a blessing? The smell of shit? No one around? A prisoner in my own house!"

"You whore, you cheap whore, where were you going—"

"Dad, stop it!"

He suddenly reached back at me, eyes wide, as if wanting to grab my shirt. I slid to the side where he couldn't get me. Betsy shrieked.

Dad pointed at Mom. "You have no appreciation. That's the problem. No appreciation! Everything is for you. Everything!"

Betsy continued her shrill shrieking. I yelled, "Stop it, Dad! Leave Mom alone!"

He reached back again, grabbing a handful of my pant leg and pulling.

"Keep your hands off them!" Mom yelled, looking at him with a fire I had not seen before.

In front of us, a pickup honked and swerved. Dad grabbed the steering wheel and jerked. The car bolted right, lifting off the ground on one side, then rumbling over the gravel shoulder before going weightless, dolls and cigarette packs and purses floating in air, heads whipping back and forth. The right front passenger side hit first, tumbling the car once, twice, before it landed on its wheels.

I awoke face up in the footwell, back hurting from the center hump. It was silent, except a faint hiss. I smelled pancakes. A green corn stalk stuck through the back window. I pulled it off me. I pushed myself up, reacquainting myself with each limb as I did, finding everything working. Corn towered around the car. Mom's head hung out her window, Dad rested on the dashboard. Betsy was not in the back seat. A stranger in a flannel shirt and cowboy hat looked in the window.

After a short search, the men from the pickup found Betsy lying in the ditch in a nest of tall grass as if sleeping. Miraculously, she hadn't broken a thing. Mom got it the worst, with a smashed spleen plus lots of bumps and bruises on her face. Dad had a concussion and a broken arm, and me, I had a concussion and a sore back but seemed otherwise fine. Eventually, I would have endless back problems, but at the time I walked away.

My Chicago grandparents came and sat with my mom in the hospital. We never visited. After a couple weeks, Granddad and Grandma arrived at the farm to pack suitcases, and there was a good deal of yelling. Dad could have saved his breath—Audrey, the pretty Chicago girl so out of place in the cornfields, would never return to the smell of shit and loneliness.

Betsy, Dad, and I went about the new normal with very little conversation. Betsy and I went to school, did our chores, and took care of ourselves while Dad worked in the fields. Betsy and I never heard from Mom, not a call, not a postcard, and late at night, when Dad was asleep after a hard day's work, Betsy and I would confess to how much we missed Mom and her flowery dresses. Later, Mom would say she wrote every day, tried to call, and put up a heroic fight for us before and after she left for Chicago. At the time, for all we knew she had just disappeared from the earth.

And every day, as Betsy and I rode the school bus into town, we would pass Dad's prized Vista Cruiser. It was right where we had left it, across the ditch on the edge of a cornfield. As fall turned into winter, I would see it there becoming dirtier and dirtier and more and more overgrown, doors open, broken skylights looking up at nothing, until finally it was covered in snow. Then one day that spring, after the snow had melted, the dirty, twisted station wagon now rested upside down in the ditch. Apparently, the farmer whose field it was had pushed it out of the way of that year's corn planting.

I wondered if Dad had seen it.

The next day, Dad drove Betsy and me into town and put us on the Greyhound to Chicago, no luggage, no toothbrush. We looked out the tinted window of the big bus and waved, but he just walked away.

About the author:

William E. Burleson's short stories have appeared in numerous literary journals and anthologies to date, including *The New Guard* and *American Fiction 14* and *16*, as well as in *Where Tales Grip*, 2019 Scribes Valley Publishing (having placed third in the annual short story contest). He is now working on a novel, *Ahnwee Days*, the story of a small town that has seen better days and the mayor who tries to save it. Burleson has also published extensively in non-fiction, including *Hennepin History Magazine* and numerous other publications. Burleson is also the founder of Flexible Press, whose recent work includes the biography *Oromo Witness*, novel *Under Ground* and the anthologies *22 Under 22*, *Home*, and *Lake Street Days*.

For examples of past work and more information, visit: williamburleson.com.

THIRD PLACE

THE SEVENTH SCAR
©2021 by Chad V. Broughman

Many a red-hot day did Jay and Dean spend sitting on the curb by the sewer grate, listening to the foul water running below, dreaming up chancy adventures and most importantly, drumming up ways to pledge their loyalty to one another. Seems none of the typical boyhood pacts would do. Spitting and handshakes—not tough enough. A jackknife to the wrist, bleeding into one another—not original. But then came the day Dean's dad spoke to them from under the family's glossy Chevy Camaro, a strange shade of green, like parakeet feathers and seaweed. His thick, veiny hand reached out for a wrench, a steady stream of blood flowing from between his thumb and pointer finger and down his wrist. He peeked out, gave a hardy chuckle, then pulled down the sleeve of his flannel to soak up the leaking wound, saying, "It takes seven scars to be a man, boys."

The gold strike.

Jay and Dean locked eyes. Without words, they knew what they had to do. The next morning was the last day of summer and what's more, the dreaded first day of middle school. They climbed onto Dean's garage roof. Deep down, Jay knew he was only talking, that he wouldn't actually jump. But he knew Dean would. When they bickered over who was going first, Dean held out some, and it made Jay nervous. So, he called him a pussy. He was ready to badger him more, to talk about courage and honor, things he knew would roil him, but female genitalia did the trick.

They climbed the rickety wood ladder, crabbed to the roof's edge, high-top Converse peeking over, nothing but air. Then an argument erupted over a three count. Did it mean jump on "three" or was there an unspoken "four"? They finally settled on the former. With their innards wobbling like rattletraps, they crouched, ready to leap into manhood. Dean whispered, "One and two," then shouted "three!" and bounded off the garage, plummeting fifteen feet to the ground.

Both boys heard his tibia snap—Dean on the ground and Jay still standing on the roof. It was a low, vexing sound that no human part should ever make.

Jay scrambled down the rungs and hovered close by. Dean's shinbone was poking through the skin like a polished shark's tooth from an airport gift shop. The blood didn't spill out right away, so both of them stared at the white wedge, looking at each other with big eyes, waiting for something more. When the dam finally broke, it came in spurts, like someone stomping on a bunch of ketchup packets. After the sting kicked in, Dean bleated, high and shrill, begging Jay to push it back in.

For a moment, Jay stood motionless, watching his friend writhe like a baited grub. Then he snapped to, turned on his heel and ran for help. As he made his way through the yard, heading for the front of Dean's house, the pity and fear drained from him like a tire leak, slow and easy. There was some disgrace for having bailed on his could-have-been blood brother, but "Thank God it wasn't me" thrummed loudest in his brain, staving off any space for shame.

Between short puffs and weighty heaves, he managed to tell Dean's dad what had happened, the man's face thinning and paling with each hurled word. When he jolted up from the table and dashed out the door, Jay fell in behind. And then, something loosened in his guts. He felt it swivel and twist like a hungry sidewider until it landed someplace else—someplace darker and less steady. He couldn't define it. Nor could his mind measure it. Even at twelve years old, though, his sensibility could grasp the jolt of a downslide. It felt bad. And it felt for keeps. He wanted to rail against it, but he didn't know how to battle something that he couldn't even see.

Though the Fosters were re-stationed the following year, Dean never really left Jay. Every time his moral compass teetered, there was Dean—his face, his scream, his shinbone. Like when Jay cheated on the AP Calc. exam, plugged all that sine, cosine crap into his fancy new calculator. Mrs. Good never suspected a thing, but Dean flashed through his head, wispy black hair standing on end as he tumbled from the roof like a rock. Or all the times he pushed past the hunched over folks at the casino, elbowing his way into the jackpot drawings, pretending he was helping them up the stairs. And the time he turned back the odometer, selling some starving graduate student his piece-of-shit Pacer. Poof! Dean appeared, making *tsk* sounds with his tongue, wagging a disapproving finger on one hand, and the other still holding his lower leg as it bleeds out, darkening the dirt beneath.

And the insider trading.

And the Ponzi schemes.

And all of the "But it's you I love" speeches to vulnerable, bewildered lovers...

Yet the tinderbox moment came the night he betrayed his fiancé, weakness and truth colliding like a supernova, leaving nothing but a big, black, sucking hole. It was his own bachelor party when he fucked the waitress from Bob's Tavern, the one with the crooked bangs and paper-thin camisole, a faded crucifix tattoo peeking out of her thick cleavage. He didn't know her name, only that she had battered knees and egg breath. And that her baby cried in its crib nearby.

Too drunk to shower off the Aqua Net and imitation Jean Naté from the local Revco, he stumbled into bed next to his betrothed, pants at his ankles, breath of a dragon. In the morning, the note on the refrigerator read—*May you find what you're looking for—*

and the engagement ring was on the table. So, he hocked it, bought some amateur porn from Hollywood Video then drank himself into blankness at the Rusty Cog. All the while, he fought the sour memory of his father's luggage on the sidewalk, truck running, and mom standing in the window, a crumpled white shirt in her grip, lipstick other than her own smeared across the collar like blood on snow.

With his fingers tingling and his face sagging loose, Jay focused hard on staying in his lane on the trek home. But when he finally turned onto his street, that last drink, the damnable vodka Gimlet—light on the simple syrup, lime wedge the size of a tire—soaked up his brain, flipped his judgment like a switch, from a bit dim to an all-out soupy fog. When his house came into view, all perception and distance blurred. He sped directly at it, crossing end-long over the neighbor's lawn then into their driveway.

A slight bump. A low whimper. He'd crushed the hind legs of their Labrador, Max. They dragged behind the dog like kite strings as it tried inching toward the house with only front paws. Panic sliced through the alcohol like a machete. Everything was fast and frantic, yet the air turned thick, like oil seeping through his lungs. His soul told him to reach for the rags in the backseat, but instead, he grabbed the tire iron. Dean's face flickered wildly in his mind's eye as he reared the steely tool high overhead. He glanced at the house. No sign of movement, only the white, blue glow of the television splashing against the living room wall. His heart thrashed against his ribcage, pounded in his mouth, his ears. Then he turned back to the broken hound, dug his upper teeth into his lower lip, clenching his body for the kill—

A boxy SUV appeared at the entrance of the cul-de-sac. For an instant, the yellow light flooded the scene like water. And just as quickly, the vehicle turned left, disappearing behind a row of manicured Hydrangea bushes, then went dark. In that blink of time, Jay saw himself, illuminated, like the star of some brutal slasher flick. He was motionless, arm still raised like a statue from the underworld. He glanced down at the broken animal as it let out a thin mewl—eyes wide, searching, sleek as crow feathers.

"For the love of God," Jay whispered through clutched lips. "Who am I?" His chest went hollow, his legs weightless. Nerves pricked and bubbled like soda, and he let out the air he'd been holding. Slowly, the tire iron came down, his mouth dry as sand, tongue dipped in glue. He scooped Max into his arms and stumbled to the porch as if unconscious, carrying him like an offering, the trampled legs bent and drooping. He set the dog down gently and before turning away, stroked its back, the fur soft against his fat-knuckled hand. In a split second, all his filth boiled up, lodged in his throat, his neck, his arteries. Max lifted his head. And Jay was cornered, the dregs of his misdeeds like a shrinking cage.

He held back the tears as he spoke—voice cracking, words wobbly, "Sorry, ol' boy."

The sky is dark gray, the color of oyster meat. And the rain is light but constant, the grass wet and glistening. Dean's house is abandoned now. There's a "For Sale" sign in front—Beaumont Realty—hanging by a hinge, the post leaning way forward like a wayward drunkard. Spindly ragweed has overtaken the yard and porch. Jay traipses to the garage, just as threatening as four decades earlier. His pulse doubles down, pumping hard in his face. The same wooden ladder they used as kids is still hanging on the side wall. He stands it upright, shimmies the side-rails into the dirt then starts to climb, slow but deliberate, gripping each rung tight. He's more winded with each heft, partly because he's forty-eight and twenty-plus overweight, but mostly from fear of the restitution at hand. He creeps toward the edge, looks out over his youth. Across the way is his childhood home, the wood slats sided with vinyl now, shamrock green, and there's a set of saw-horses in the yard, plywood resting across them and what looks to have been a push mower, its guts strewn about like a field-dressed deer. A wave of nostalgia swells up but he snuffs it out, pulls off his shoes and tosses them aside. It feels right being barefoot. He takes another step forward. The shingles are slick but still they bite at the soft pads of his feet. He curls his toes over the eavestrough, stares down at the dampened twigs, leaves and black moss that have gathered through the seasons.

Sucking in hard, he pulls back his arms like slingshots taking aim, then bows at the waist, readying to fling himself into absolution. He counts to two in his head, hears Dean's voice shout "three" then starts to swing forward. His chest is out over the edge yet hesitation anchors his lower half.

And he slips. His backside strikes the rigid surface with a low thud. He glanced off, the trajectory in motion. Firing out his hand, Jay clutches the eavestrough. It crumples a foot or two before catching. The crunch of metal sounds out. Then, he dangles, mid-air, caught between pulling himself up—or letting go—

About the author:

Chad V. Broughman was the recipient of the Rusty Scythe Prize Book award in 2016 and in 2017 was awarded the Adobe Cottage Writers Retreat honor in New Mexico. As well, Chad was awarded a chapbook contract for his collection of short stories, "the forsaken," which was published by Etchings Press. His fiction can be found in journals nationwide—such as *Carrier Pigeon, East Coast Literary Review, River Poets Journal, Burningword, Pulp Fiction, Sky Island Journal,* and *From Whispers to Roars*—and he has been anthologized in the Write Michigan Short Story Anthology and On Loss, an anthology. He is a Best of the Net and Pushcart Prize nominee, holds an MFA from Spalding University and served as co-editor for the fiction/poetry blog 'Cafe Aphra' based out of the United Kingdom. Chad teaches English and Creative Writing at the secondary and post-secondary levels and is a husband to the grooviest wife on the planet as well as the proud father of two rambunctious young sons.

IT IS WHAT IT ISN'T
©2021 by Thomas Maurstad

Dread, like a bomb blast, flattened everything. He couldn't think anything else—no desperate plans, no frantic schemes. He couldn't feel anything else—first there had been shock, which had almost immediately metastasized into panic. But now? Just the dread.

He walked through the parking garage, never looking up or turning his head. He heard the click of his car unlocking. He dropped his satchel on the passenger seat, slid in, and shut the door. He started the car and punched off the stereo the instant it came on. Then he sat, gripping the steering wheel, staring straight ahead, and listened to himself breathe as he tried to muster a pep talk to bully himself into some sort of bullshit buoyancy.

He thought of Gerald. His smile twitched into a wince as he brought up his phone, and there was the text he had felt buzz against his chest earlier during...all that.

Stopped for takeout at Royal China on the way home. See you soon?

Gerald. Home. See you. Soon. And here came another wave of dread. He didn't want to stay. He didn't want to go. There was The Before and there was The After. He was in The After. Gerald was still in The Before. Soon Gerald would join him in The After. As soon as he got home. As soon as Gerald saw him. As soon as their eyes met. Soon.

He watched his knuckles whiten as he squeezed the steering wheel and imagined Gerald puttering about, working on whatever checklist tasks he'd brought home with him. Letting the dog out or, by this time, letting her back in and feeding her. He smiled and then winced again as he pictured this scene, sweet and doomed. He glanced at his watch. This time of day his drive home would take about twenty minutes, no more than half an hour, unless...unless...unless.... Now he simultaneously winced and chuckled. What? Was he about to wish for a pile-up on the tollway or maybe a flat tire? He shook his head and started to back out of the space.

A horn blast shattered his isolation; he stomped on the brake pedal. He hadn't looked back, but now he did. The side of a dirty white van filled his rear window. He lowered his window, stuck out an arm, waved his apologies, and received another rat-tat-tat of horn blasts. The van roared off with a belch of blue exhaust. Deep breath. Rearview mirror. Turn to double-check. He backed out, exited the parking garage, and turned toward the tollway.

His heart beat high in his chest, threatening to bounce up into his throat. Taillights streamed past on either side. He tried to make his eyes go soft, turn all those red dots into neon ribbons like an open-exposure photograph. Big, ruddy moon just above the horizon. That's right. Blood Moon tonight. Any other night, he would have called Gerald to say, "Honey, go out on the deck and look at the moon," and listened as Gerald did. "So beautiful." "It is, isn't it?" "Be home soon."

Any other night.

He was turning onto his street. How did that happen? He didn't remember taking the exit, or the six-seven-eight traffic lights and now this last of two-three-four stop signs. Five more blocks, right turn, crunch down the gravel driveway, into the carport, step on slate stones through the yard, up one-two-three steps onto the deck and through the sliding glass door, whereupon Daisy would clamor to greet him as Gerald came from the kitchen to join in. And as he did, Gerald would look at him and...and...and....

He saw two amber rings floating beside a black sedan parked along the curb. It took a moment to realize they were the eyes of a cat staring into his headlights as his car approached. What might he have imagined those cat eyes were in that moment before recognition? Thinking of silly possibilities—mating fireflies, tiny twin black holes—would have offered a brief break from the dread pressing on his chest, squeezing his insides, making his thighs ache. No chance. Just as his front tires came even with the black sedan, the cat dashed under his car.

There was a quick series of muffled knocks, like a sneaker tumbling in a dryer. It was over even as he realized it was happening, and by the time he reacted, he was half a block down the street. He rested his forehead on the steering wheel. It was quiet, for a moment. All he heard was his car engine's steady idle. But then a wild yowl rose up from behind. He looked in his rearview mirror and shuddered. The cat was flipping and cartwheeling in the middle of the street, a spastic dance as life convulsed into death. He watched. He wanted to look away. He wanted to *want* to look away. He didn't look away.

I should go back and see what I can do, he thought. The cat's yowl grew raspier as the arc of its flips flattened.

Going.

"Why did it do that?" he asked out loud. The cat let out a long, guttural groan. No more flips. It flopped on its side and stayed there.

Going.

There was nothing I could do, he thought. *It happened so...it was all...perfect. There's no avoiding or evading a perfect moment.* He spoke his conclusion out loud, "If you could, it wouldn't be." The cat was silent and still.

Gone.

He drove on. He wasn't driving the car; he was watching himself drive the car. He watched himself look at the moon again, over the trees in his neighbor's yard—a higher, smaller smudge. He watched himself pull into their carport and turn off the car and grab his satchel and get out of the car and close the door. He watched himself walk across slate stones and up one-two-three steps and stop before the sliding-glass door.

Here came Daisy. He slid the door open and stepped in. Here

came Gerald. He bent over and devoted himself to reciprocating Daisy's enthusiastic greeting. As long as he was bent over, he didn't have to look at Gerald and Gerald wouldn't know. But he had to straighten and he had to look.

So, he did. Gerald was almost beside him, just another couple steps. Gerald was looking down at his phone and now was looking up. Their eyes met. He felt his face flush as he smiled. He waited for Gerald's expression to change, his eyes to widen, his smile to freeze. But...nothing. Now Gerald was next to him, saying something about the construction that had screwed up his drive home every day this week and then reminding him about the fundraiser they had promised Lee and Roderick they would attend tomorrow night.

Kiss.

"And how was your day?

Gerald's hazel eyes were so sweetly crinkled. Daisy's tail whumped against his calf.

"Fine. Good."

Tomorrow. One more night. Tomorrow.

"Let's eat. I'm famished."

He took a step toward the kitchen. And the dread pressed on.

About the author:

Thomas Maurstad was the pop culture critic of the *Dallas Morning News* for over 20 years. Since his release back into the wild, he is endeavoring to create ambitious, compelling fiction.

TALKING TREES AND CHORUS LEAVES
©2021 by Joseph J. Salerno

I call him Mr. Beech, if he is a *he* at all. I am told by a friend who happens to know of trees that Mr. Beech grows both male and female flowers, which, I suppose, makes him a sort of hermaphrodite, AC/DC, inter-trans-whatever. I just call him Mr. Beech.

He greets me most mornings as I step out onto my second-floor fire escape, my "veranda," for early coffee. He is securely planted about thirty feet away at the back edge of the graveled yard, and he stretches about forty feet high and easily as wide.

He is an American Beech, *fagus grandifolia*, and his main purpose is to listen to my complaints and confessions, as well as to provide me with oxygen. In exchange, I simply promise not to stare at his lady-friend, Ms. Maple, his red-leaved paramour planted directly behind him, just a few feet away, across the fence on the adjoining property. She's a beauty. He knows I love redheads, and his broad branches shield most of her from my sight.

My veranda is the side of a fire escape with a cement slab floor of six by eight feet. I utilize it as a porch, with a three-tiered planter of basil, chives, and parsley in the corner; a few tomato plants in pots near the black metal staircase going to the third floor; and a small, white, round cocktail table in the middle flanked by two chairs. No complaints from the Village Fire Marshall yet, but I have only been living here for sixteen years.

Mr. Beech finds me this morning at the white cocktail table with a stack of twelve bank statements I agreed to work on at home for my boss, who is a CPA. The clickety-clack of the calculator printer as I add columns down and then across accompanies the chirping of birds.

"Dammit!" I yell, after about forty-five minutes of crunching. "Exactly eight freaking dollars off!" I stare at Mr. Beech in the early morning sunshine and sip some coffee. I peruse the twelve sheets of numbers, not even knowing where to search for the error.

Mr. Beech, in his wisdom, with his light-green ovate spaded leaves, whispers:

"You just added deposits and then withdrawals of about two-and-a-half million dollars. They don't totally correlate. Eight dollars. Hmmm. I suppose eights and zeros can look very much alike; you may have confused one for the other. I think eight bucks, considering, is well within a decent margin of error."

Those very words enter my head as I sit and stare at Mr. Beech. He is right, of course. I will later ask Phil, my boss, whether eight dollars is, indeed, within a decent margin of error.

"Thank you, Mr. Beech. Eight bucks, zero bucks, we'll just have to fudge through."

Lorenzo, my thirty-something nephew, descends the fire escape stairs from the third floor, where he resides. He wishes me a good morning and hands me a mug of gourmet joe.

"I'm usually good with just Folgers, you know."

"Loosen up. This is better. You're welcome."

I take a sip and smile a smile of gratitude. Lorenzo looks sharp, slicked-back black hair, pressed shirt, tie, and slacks. I assume his jacket is probably still upstairs. We sit and enjoy the coffee.

"Lookin' spiffy," I say. "Anything special going on today?"

"Nothing that special," he replies. "Just showing a few newbies how to work the new software. And you?" He glances at the monthly bank statements. "Frannie's Boxes, Incorporated. What the hell do they do?"

"Shipping equipment, I think, but not too big time. S-Corporation, relatively small potatoes." I look out at Mr. Beech. "It sure is a beautiful day."

"Yeah, it is a beautiful day," echoes my nephew. "You seeing

Marion today?"

I find the question a bit leading. "Probably. Should I send her your regards?"

"You know, Uncle Rollo, you should really—" but he stops right there. He is about to give me the same old speech about getting out of the "Friendship Zone" and actually getting serious with Marion. He has directed me to a few, or *ten*, of those six-minute videos on YouTube describing techniques for going from friendship to love affair. Problem is, those videos are there to make you subscribe, to make money, and my nephew is there just to prove he gives great advice. His own love-life is scattered and quite shallow, and I cherish Marion's friendship. Not to be jeopardized.

"Uncle Rollo, what's in that pot with, like, dirt but no plant in it?" He points to a small clay pot down on the floor near the table.

"I made some lemonade with actual lemons a few days ago and planted the lemon seeds. Should shoot up in this warm weather within a week."

"Lemon seeds? From *lemons*? You don't need to buy the seeds from the store?"

When I realize he is being serious, I kinda feel sorry for how out of touch he is. *Seeds from the store*. Really?

"It might be time to finish your coffee," I say. "This is good stuff, thank you. I'm sure those newbies will have an excellent instructor. "

Lorenzo sits there, finishes sipping his coffee, and hesitates, as if he has more to say.

"What?" I ask.

"The 'Friendship Zone,' Uncle Rollo, the 'Friendship Zone.' Get out of it. You deserve better."

"Don't forget the coffee mug. Thank you."

Lorenzo quickly walks up the stairs.

"Impertinent little twerp," observes Mr. Beech. "If up to me, I would trim some of his limbs."

"That's not—doable—not in the human world, Mr. Beech."

"You sound like you agree with the young chainsaw."

"I don't totally disagree. It's called ambivalence—mixed feelings. He may be wrong; he may be right. In any case, we humans generally strive not to squash the younger generation's opinions and feelings. It is our way."

"Ah, if you only knew," says Mr. Beech. "If you only knew of the countless squashed saplings that lay dried-up and gone at my feet due to my grand foliage. My younger generations need to float and fly and find their own piece of land and sun."

"Mr. Beech, I've gotta go soon, we'll talk later. Regards to Ms. Maple."

"She's been given many regards, thank you very much. Mind your manners."

Fagus grandifolia. Jealous old fogey.

I wish I could say that the office is as pleasant an atmosphere as my sunshiny veranda, but it is not. Besides the fact that the walls are stark white and the desks are white laminate and the computer hardware and screens are black plastic and the carpet is industrial-grade blue, there is also "Phil's Directive." Phil, being the boss, demands that no plants or aquarium fish or any living things beside personnel inhabit said office. It is cleaned twice a week, and the desks always smell like lemon Clorox, the carpets always smell like lemon Renuzit carpet powder, and the air is always lemon Lysol-ed. Lemons from the store, indeed.

I am immediately told to get the totals for the twelve monthly bank statements for Frannie's Boxes, Incorporated to add up and correlate, even if it takes a few hours. I go over to the water jug and drink a few cups of cold water, and enjoy the *glub-glub* of the rising air bubbles. I am about to take a cup of water to my desk, when I remember another of Phil's Directives. "No drinking liquids at the desks." I swallow a third cup of water and trash the plastic.

Despite my feelings on the sterility of the atmosphere, the rest of the day goes fairly smoothly. I finally *do* get Frannie's Boxes,

Incorporated to jive, I review a few more years of various company bank statements, and I go through the worksheet on taxable Social Security Benefits for one of Phil's elderly clients. The scent of lemons in the office keeps reminding me of Lorenzo. "From lemons? You don't need to buy the seeds from the store?"

Marion calls me in mid-afternoon. She asks if I am interested in sharing a pizza for dinner, a large pie with mushrooms and onions. She would bring it over to my apartment, and we could have it on my veranda at six-ish. I agree to it, hoping there is to be no "pop-in" from my third-floor neighbor.

By a quarter to six I am home, showered and shaved and at the white cocktail table with a pitcher of ice water and a radio tuned to an FM station playing classic rock.

"Gotta date, Mr. Beech. Marion's coming over, so be on your best behavior." The wide swaying tree gives no answer, still angry at my "Regards to Ms. Maple" comment. "Marion is coming over," I repeat, but he is still pissed-off. "Oh, be that way!"

Marion arrives at about six-ten, with the pie and a bottle of cold Pinot Grigio.

"This basil is lovely," she remarks, and she picks about a dozen large leaves, goes into the kitchen to rinse them off and chop them into small bits, and then she sprinkles them onto the warm pizza. "Now *that* is a proper pizza pie."

"For an Irishwoman, you sure know your Italian cuisine."

"Now, Roland. Hello, Mr. Beech!" She waves to the tree. "Has he been spouting any wisdom lately?" she asks me.

"Tons. But right now, he's a bit upset at me. Don't ask me why."

"You are the only person I know who talks to trees," she says, as she takes a bite of pizza. "And then you get them upset. How does that work?"

I just shrug.

"It *is* a beautiful evening, though," she says.

"Even more beautiful with you and the wine," I say, kissing her on the cheek. "That was for the wine—and *you*."

"Well," she changes gears, "Your basil and parsley are magnificent, the chives look good, and the tomatoes are in flower. I've never seen a fire escape so—well-adorned. What's in the pot with dirt?"

I quote lyrics from the silly sixties song about how lemon trees are pretty and their flowers are sweet, but you can't eat their fruit.

"Lemon tree? Interesting. Would it survive the winter?"

"It isn't something I have given much thought to. I suppose on a sunny windowsill, it might. I'd be happy just to see it spring up a bit."

"I'm sure it will," she says. After she finishes her second slice, she informs me that she has promised to join her daughter in a hatha yoga class later this very evening.

"You're kidding? I thought we were going to watch a DVD. I finally get hold of the DiCaprio *The Great Gatsby* and...I dunno. I just can't see you in a yoga class."

"Liz's idea. I promise, I'll come back tomorrow. We'll get to Gatsby. I'll just light up one last Newport, help you finish this wine, and go."

"I'll miss you. I'm not watching it alone."

"I know."

After she leaves, I put the four leftover pizza slices in the fridge and the empty wine bottle in the recycling bin. I sit on the veranda with a snifter of Jack Daniels, thinking, "That is some way to show up to a yoga class, with pizza, wine, and nicotine in your system."

At almost eight p.m., it is still bright out. "How you doing out there, Mr. Beech?" There is no answer from the tree, but there arises a slight murmur from the basil leaves.

"A very presumptuous woman," shouts the Chorus of Sweet Basil, *ocimum basilicum*. "She could have at least asked you before picking at our leaves."

"No harm done," I reply. "It is your purpose to sweeten and aromatize my food. She just did what I would have done."

The Basil Chorus has more to say. "As presumptuous as she is, we have given her much thought. We concur with your nephew;

we feel strongly that your relationship needs to get to the next level. Are you content with just pizza and wine?"

"What's going on here, Basil? I need this advice right now like I need a third armpit. I'm no spring chicken, you know. Last time I was with a woman, she was twenty years younger. Freakin' disaster. I don't know why I'm telling *you* this, you're like a damn Greek Chorus, moralizing, cathartic, brooding. I admire your look and your aroma, Basil, but that's about it! Just jazz up my food and sauces, make some decent pesto, and we'll get along."

Mr. Beech, though still angry with me, suddenly interrupts. "My dear Basil, we're just gonna have to cut this human some slack. They come and go so often; they often don't even *know* whether they're coming or going. Leave him to his poison drink."

"Hey! Come on, Mr. Beech!"

The Chorus of Basil gets in a final encouraging and subservient word. "We believe in you, human. We will serve, garnish, and aromatize. Tomorrow is another day." As the sun goes down, the trees and the herbs fall silent. They do not communicate with me past sundown.

I sit there with my snifter of Jack Daniels. I am glad and content that liquor, for the limited use I make of it, does not talk back to me. I am in no need of any more opinions and points-of-view from other bizarre sources.

About the author:

Born and raised in Brooklyn, New York, Joseph Salerno is the product of twelve years of Catholic School, after which he attended Columbia for three years. After a variety of occupations (Title Searcher, Architectural Draftsman, et. al), he has settled on being an Office Manager for a small accounting firm.

Joseph has a degree in Psychology from SUNY Empire State College. An avid short story reader and writer, he is a member of The Long Island Writer's Guild. He has self-published twelve chapbooks of short stories in the past eight years.

Joseph's work has appeared in *Guilders '84: The Literary Magazine of Hofstra University* (1984), *Open Minds Quarterly* (2014), and he was a finalist for the short story prize in Scribes Valley Publishing's 2019 anthology: *Where Tales Grip*.

He lives with about a dozen large house plants in an apartment three blocks from the New York City limits.

THE GREAT DIVIDE
©2021 by Scott Pedersen

Heading home, satisfied that our customer was satisfied, I crisscrossed the Great Divide several times until I approached a succinct sign: SCENIC OVERLOOK. The highway department wouldn't lie, would they? Under some circumstances, sure they would. I pulled onto the pea-gravel surface, grabbed the green book that had been sliding around on the front seat, and got out of my car.

The book belonged to Royce, the owner of the custom-electronics company I worked for. At a meeting in his living room, I'd feigned interest in the old volume. Royce tossed it into my lap as if it were a cheap comic book. "Read it on the trip. Who knows? It could change your life."

Casual profundity suited him. I once asked him why he never locked his car. He said he didn't want to live like that, that he'd rather take the chance of something bad happening and live life the way it ought to be lived. At the time I thought he was delusional, but in the five years I'd known him, I'd never seen anything bad happen to him. Maybe he was on to something. On the other hand, maybe it just hadn't caught up with him yet.

Now, seated on a weathered bench, with an eastward panorama inspiring me to appreciate where I was—the highway department had told the truth, this time—I raised the book from my lap. Its title was embossed in gold leaf on the leather front cover: *Ta Tung (The Great Harmony)*. It surprised me that Confucius wrote books. I flipped to a random page, which told of a future where *"...selfish schemings are repressed, and robbers, thieves and other lawless men no longer exist, and there is no need for people to shut their outer doors."* That intrigued me enough to read more, and I found that this passage was part of his description of an ideal society, albeit one tricked out in Eastern values I'd always shrugged off.

I closed the book and looked up. A vast, multihued patchwork of land stretched out before me. Above it was a boundless sky flecked with hawks buoyed by warm updrafts to heights that would thrill even a bird of prey. The planet looked for the first time like a place where such an ideal society could exist. Here, at the top of a continent, I was far removed from all selfish schemings, and within my sight were no lawless men, nor any people at all.

With the sun now setting, I drove on to the mountaintop lodge where I'd reserved a room. There I settled into my soft bed for a night of comfortable and deep sleep.

I woke up early, as usual. I tugged open the curtains to reveal a gray day, a heavy blanket of stratus clouds hiding the sky. I quickly packed up and headed down to the first floor.

Before checking out, I grabbed a sweet roll from the breakfast bar. I would have taken a yogurt, but they were sitting out. Who knows for how long?

The drive home was long, with hairpin turns slowing my progress down the mountains. Then the sheer distance on the plains kept me dulled with boredom. I arrived home in mid-afternoon, planning to relax the rest of the day. A phone call from Royce interfered. He wanted to hear about my trip, saying he couldn't wait until the next day.

I met him at Tomasino's, a restaurant where we'd often go to talk business. Royce said it was a tax deduction. I was on board with that—anything to starve the beast.

We sat in a booth. It was a tight squeeze for him, stretching his lime-green T-shirt to one side. I noticed his normally shaggy mustache had been trimmed, revealing for the first time a delicate upper lip.

Royce was a nodder. He'd nod at anything, like he was cool with whatever might happen. A client once told him a major job we'd counted on was cancelled. Royce sat there nodding. He even thanked the guy.

As soon as our food arrived, he started peppering me. Was the client still planning to expand? How much more business could we expect from them? All pretty uninteresting to me, being a technology guy.

Then he said something surprising. "So, what did you think of Andrea and her crew? I had a great time with them when I was there."

"What? You told me you'd never been there."

"Oh, that was just a white lie. I thought it would be good for you to meet them in person, since you seemed a bit skeptical—I still don't know why—and just to take a trip. Expand your horizons. You're so preplanned. I'd love to see you do something spontaneous just once."

"Well, please don't do that again."

He seemed undeterred. "So, not a bad bunch of people over there, right?"

"I don't know about that. I was focused on the work. Once they all shut up, I was able to install the upgrades."

He nodded. "So, what did you think of the book?"

"I liked it. Sorry I forgot to bring it with me. I have it locked up at home. I thought it might be valuable."

"Could be. I wouldn't know, because I stole it."

"Stole it?"

"Yeah, the store owner was just oblivious, with his head buried in some old book. Hey, don't look at me like that. It was a long time ago, and I was a different person then. I'd send the book back, but they're out of business now."

"Because of all the shoplifting?"

"You know, I've really taken that book to heart. Basically, it's about being generous. Maybe sometimes things won't go my way, but I believe at the end of my life I'll be a richer person for it."

"That last part makes it sound selfish."

He nodded. "I must not be explaining it right. Look, I'll pick up the check if you leave the tip. How does that sound?"

"Sounds good. Thanks."

After we finished eating, I dropped six dollar bills—I was pretty sure I counted six—onto the table for a tip. After putting on my jacket, I looked again. There were only five. I decided against saying something, not wanting to make a stink over a dollar. Now that I knew he was a thief; I would keep my guard up in the future.

A couple hours later someone was pounding on my front door. Royce waved through the window. Now what did he want?

I turned on the porch light. Royce shielded his eyes and shouted, "Hey, can I get that book?" I hesitated but then opened the door. He stepped inside. "I was having a beer with my brother around the corner, and I thought since I was this close...."

This whole thing with the book was starting to sound like one of those selfish schemes it talked about. That would explain why he was so eager for me to borrow it. It would give him an excuse to get into my house. I shouldn't have told him I locked it up—now he probably thought I had other valuables. I would have to be careful. "I'll get it. You can wait here."

"Wow! What's with all the deadbolts?" He started flipping the levers of my front door locks. "You know, Carl, I don't think there's been a burglary in this neighborhood since Calvin Coolidge was president."

"So, I guess everybody's deadbolts have been working."

"Funny, Carl. But isn't this a bit low-tech for you?"

"I'm going to go electronic. I just haven't gotten around to it. Wait here. I'll get the book."

I entered my office, a converted bedroom. Royce stepped in a second later.

"I locked it in my file cabinet. I'll get it. Just stay here," I said as I stepped around him and opened the door to the small walk-in closet I used for storage. The heavy-duty file cabinet took up almost half the space.

The closet darkened as Royce's massive body filled the doorway. It was too dark to see his face, but I was sure he was smirking, knowing how intimidated a scrawny guy like me would be with him towering over me and blocking my only possible escape. I pulled the string that turned on the overhead light and unlocked the cabinet.

Without thinking, I pulled the top drawer toward me, another mistake on my part. The first thing revealed were a few of my jars of gold coins. I'd been buying them, mostly Krugerrands, for years. My father used to say, "In gold we trust." He knew what he was talking about.

Royce's breathing was suddenly audible. He stepped closer. "Are those gold? Holy shit! You should keep those in a safe deposit box."

"They're fine here."

How would he have reacted if he'd seen all the other jars I kept in the lower drawers? Now that he knew, what was there to keep him from breaking into my house while I was on my next trip?

When the drawer was fully open, I picked up the book from the back and handed it to him. I wished I hadn't. I'd forgotten about my revolver, which was now in plain view.

Royce's breathing got louder. "Is that a Ruger Blackhawk? I used to target practice with one. It had a steel grip instead of aluminum. What's this one got?"

He reached for the gun, his belly pushing the drawer in. I had to act fast. There would be no stopping him once he was armed. I plunged my hand into the drawer, grabbed the gun, and pressed it into his chest. The green cotton of his shirt puckered around the barrel.

I looked up at his face. Again with the nodding!

I pushed the gun harder.

He stopped nodding. "What are you trying to do, Carl? Show me you can be spontaneous? Don't fool around." He raised an open hand toward the gun.

I'd never fired the gun before and was surprised at the recall. I felt my wrist ache as he fell on top of me.

I expected to have little trouble with the grand jury. All I had to do was tell the truth, which I had gone over in my mind again and again until I could have told the story in my sleep: Royce showed up at my house drunk and demanding that I give him his book back. He then forced his way into my storage closet, tricked me into opening the file cabinet, and immediately reached for the gun, which accidentally discharged as we struggled over it. It all matched what I'd told the police that night.

The odd thing was that the DA didn't seem very interested in the events of that evening. She was more interested in that damn book. She wanted to know exactly how it came into my possession, which I explained, and asked me to describe my dinner with Royce. I told her everything, just as I had explained to the police. I said he asked about my trip and talked about being generous.

She stopped me after I said he had stolen the book. She held up a piece of paper. "This is a handwritten receipt the police found inside the book. It shows that Royce Williams purchased the book for thirty-five dollars from Schuler Books. We contacted the owner, who remembered the transaction and even described Mr. Williams in detail."

Now, even though I'd been honest from the start, my credibility had taken a hit. Maybe the jury wouldn't believe the rest of my testimony, all because of another lie of Royce's. In the end, they voted not to indict me. I figured they were just too confused by what happened. I still don't understand it. Maybe Royce wanted to impress me, make me think he'd been one of those lawless men, a selfish schemer, who'd reformed himself.

It doesn't matter. I can see the takeaway of the whole thing clearly. He was the guy who didn't lock his car door, and I'm the guy with the deadbolts. Which one of us is still alive?

About the author:

Scott Pedersen is a writer based in Wisconsin. His stories have appeared in *Louisiana Literature*, *The MacGuffin* and many other literary journals and anthologies. When not writing fiction, he enjoys performing in a traditional Celtic band.

STAR-SPANGLED GO-KART
©2021 by Steve Putnam

Percussion; the drummer on snares, another playing tom-toms. Anguished, other-worldly vocals fade. Music's always part of Anja's therapy. Riding wooden horses is the part that seems strange. First session, Dee and I had questions. "What does rocking-horse riding have to do with couples therapy?" Dee asked. "It seems more like performance art."

"Wooden horses without hoofbeat and heartbeat seems a bit offbeat," Anja admits. "Inventor called them *Equicizers*, by the way."

"Seriously?" I ask.

"You're always serious. A jockey named Lovato invented the Equicizer. Riders use it to warm up, train, or ride off-season. It was used to film close-ups for that movie, *Seabiscuit*. It gives horses a well-deserved break."

"Will horses become more useless if everyone takes up riding these contraptions?"

"So far, that's not a problem."

Oblivious to the beat, Woody, Woodward, and Forester stare woodenly, standing eye to eye, face to face. We saddle our wooden horses and mount up.

"Are we jousting today?" I ask.

"Eyes are gateways." Anja smiles. "Face to face, we can search each other's souls."

"Where are we going with that?" I ask.

Dee's voice is solemn, "Strobe, tell Anja about the star-spangled go-kart."

"What about it?" Anja asks.

"Strobe says it's just a dream. An Amerikan dream, spelled with a k."

Anja turns to me, tugging Woody's reins lightly as if that's what keeps him from colliding with Woodward. "Star-Spangled?" she asks. "Is that okay, Strobe?"

"Friend Jay worked the night shift at the corner Texaco station. There weren't many customers out and about. Locals—college students off for the summer, Vietnam vets back home, kids who didn't know which draft numbers would come up next. We all hung out. You had to wait your turn to pull your muscle car into the wash bay.

"Everyone took turns driving a go-kart, circling the gas pump island, an American flag attached to its roll bar, flapping in the breeze. The flag was small, the kind you plant on a vet's grave. Driver had to watch out for gas customers, startled by an oversize teen or undergrown adult dwarfing a go-kart. Driving in circles seemed to miraculously help college kids forget the draft, help vets forget the war they fought in, help live life before it was too late.

"I was in college on the GI bill, off for the summer, working as a GM mechanic. Jay was working nights, going to community college on and off."

"So, you are a vet?" Anja asks.

"I worked at the same Texaco station a couple of years earlier. I was bouncing from job to job. A Navy guy older than me was a customer. He must have known I was afflicted with an impaired sense of direction. He drove me to the recruiter. After boot camp, I volunteered for riverboat duty in Vietnam, an option that as far as odds go, looked to be as safe as driving drunk. It wasn't that I believed in the rightness or wrongness of that war. Instead of shooting people, I could be an engineman below decks. Some Navy paper-pusher ignored my naïve wish and assigned me to an aircraft carrier. I was supposed to work in a boiler room. But I had taken typing in high school as a joke, so I ended up working as a yeoman. I didn't object. I never volunteered for anything again. I escaped Vietnam without running away."

Anja's looking outward, eyes wide open, she's focused on me. Somehow, without me noticing, she has stopped Woody in his tracks. I feel his wooden stare.

"After serving a short, undistinguished two years honorably, I cashed in on the G.I. bill, Uncle Sam's scholarship for lucky vets who served in safe places, for combat vets lucky enough not to die. Some made up for lost civilian time, rejecting the so-called American way, evils of war, capitalism, and teeny-bopper music. I grew a beard and grew my hair long. Freedom redefined, justified a carefree sense of responsibility. In a world gone bad, you should only do what you want to do.

"Summer ended. Jay the drummer's draft number came up. Instead of community college, he went off to boot camp. At his going-away party, he played drums. Kid brother played kazoo. He returned home from boot camp, told how drill instructors build character. They'd insult recruits' mothers, march them into a tear gas-filled room, make them take off their masks, recite name rank and serial number. Standing next to his '57 Chevy, its blue paint rust-patched and primed flat black, he said he might not come back. 'Of course, you'll be back,' I said. As far as I knew, only soldiers you *don't* know die in Vietnam. Kids you know get drunk, die in car wrecks.

"His platoon was ambushed on patrol, he was the first in town to return in a box, containing the nightmare of his remains, along with the usual broken dreams, never the new muscle car, never marriage, or free college on the GI Bill."

I pause, take a breath. "I remember a townie who had joined the National Guard. 'Stupid letting myself get drafted,' the weekend warrior said. Not so. Jay did what he thought he had to do: Go to prison and dishonor his family, or face the so-called music and take the chance he might not make it back. Right or wrong, Civil Obedience saved someone further down the lottery list to pay a price unearned."

Anja keeps Woody's reins taut. Lifeless horse plods along, too depressed to tolerate talk of death. "I'm sorry," she says. "Bad time to suggest life's not fair."

"At calling hours, I tried to pay shallow respects, wishing there was something I could say. At a loss, I told the family I was sorry, one by one. Jay's father, mother, younger sister, and brothers. What else could I say: 'Some do, some don't, some go, some don't'? In after-death silence, everyone returns to work, to college. Parents set up a music scholarship in his memory. Even so, word has it Jay's mother can't cure her bouts of crying. Sister tells me a younger brother has nightmares, wakes in the middle of the night, yells out for his brother.

"Between semesters, I visited Jay's parents. Small talk seemed smaller than usual. Parents asked me about my health; I asked about theirs. We were all fine it turns out; conversation goes nowhere. TV special interrupts the strained silence. Commander in Chief, President of the United States delivers a speech pushing the people to support our men. Thanks to great American medical science and the helicopter, we have only lost thirteen thousand soldiers, he says. Jay's father retreats to the kitchen. As if hiding from an ambush, he reaches under the kitchen sink, grabs a bottle of whiskey, takes a swallow. President doesn't stop talking. Jay's father makes a call, tells someone at the other end of the phone line to take the president off the air. I still remember the rage, his insistence, his wife silent, embarrassed."

Woody's not missing a beat. Anja blinks her eyes a couple of times, head not turned enough to hide from me. "That's sad. His family had little choice but to keep going. Dog and pony politician reminding them of loss they're trying to forget. Politician who never served reminds Americans safe in front of their TVs, 'Support the troops; support the war.'"

"There's wasn't anything more to say. Not only is small talk small, but it's also hard to pull off. I was afraid I was as bad as the TV, reminding Jay's parents of things that could no longer be. Better to move on.

"All said and done, Jay was one of the bystanders who saw me crying the day my horse died. He never told anyone at school, as far as I know. He could have gotten a lot of mileage out of that one."

"What could Jay have done differently? "Anja asks.

"If you pretend you can't hear, draft physical doc drops a dime on the floor to see if you turn to look. Flunking a hearing test would have been a big pass. Aside from skipping military service, nothing good or bad happens. Oppose war as a Conscientious Objector. Vets sometimes resented COs, thought they should get their asses shot at too. Best they could do to make things right, tune-up the CO, wait for the bruises to heal, rough him up again."

With Anja's assistance, Woody picks up the pace. "Any upside?" she asks.

"Tremendous opportunity to combine education with life experience. Attend college on a ROTC scholarship, major in political science. Draft triggered a brief resurgence in American family values. The rhythm method, a paradoxical form of birth control, increased odds of pregnancy, a good excuse for marriage, save a boyfriend from the draft. At least for a few years, wedlock was an escape from warlock."

"Sad or mad, you're cynical."

Dee has Forester walking at a pace slower than I thought a wooden horse could walk.

Woody is motionless, Anja looks spellbound "What a mixed message the dead unwittingly present," she says. "Just as patriots believe freedom justifies sacrifice, pacifists believe too much sacrifice justifies peace."

"Who stops to think, someone else wouldn't exist if the drummer refused to go? What if another man died in his place, never to be a parent, the unborn child ineligible to win a scholarship, or lose a draft lottery? Few remember who he was or what it was that was taken. Does anyone wonder what he thought, did, or didn't believe? Or wonder if giving up a drummer, halfway across the world, was worth it?"

"Our hourglass ran out of sand; it's time to end our session," Anja says, her voice soft, reverent. "Some do, some don't. Some go, some don't. It was a lottery, ending in a crapshoot, even if you volunteered. So, you didn't see any action. What do you say on those rare occasions when someone thanks you for your service?

I look downward. "I can't take credit for things I didn't do. Instead of saying you're welcome, I say nothing good or bad happened. Sorry, it takes me back."

"You make it sound like a yesterday."

"Yesterday a long time ago."

"Are you ashamed?" Anja asks. I don't have an answer. "Enough, we'll wait for another time." Slowly, reverently, she dismounts from Woody, picks up a jar of sunflower seeds from a nearby shelf. She reaches out. "Would you like a few?" she asks.

Hard to know what to say. I picture one of the guys driving the go-kart, a vet who looks like a Bible picture of white Jesus, long hair, bearded. He's intense, in a zone, as if going in circles can make visions of burning a village disappear. While waiting for their turns to drive, a couple of guys share a joint, killing time, waiting for Uncle Sam to pull the next lottery numbers.

I hear sounds of a four-cycle engine as the go-kart continues circling the gas pumps, American flag waving, caught in the undertow, like wastewater circling the drain. Anja's music rocks on. Bass drum throbbing a steady four-four beat; electric guitar crying a cry sadder than a gentle weep.

About the author:

Steve Putnam lives in Western Massachusetts, in ancestral shadows of farmers, carpenters, and ice dealers. He has worked as a laborer, G.M. mechanic, framing carpenter. In the last gig as a copier tech, he worked in schools, prisons, hospitals, and a scrap yard or two. Putnam also guest-starred as a copier repairman under the corporate florescence of a large life insurance company. He often paddles marathon canoes, solo or tandem with his wife, Cynthia.

His novels "Academy of Reality," and "Loose Horse Lost," both made finalist lists in the 2019 Faulkner-Wisdom Competition in New Orleans. His short fiction has appeared in *Carbon Culture Review* online, *Whiskey Island* online, as well as Scribes Valley Anthologies: *Beyond the Norm* (2018) "Seltzer Can on a Blue Tractor Painted Orange"; *Where Tales Grip* (2019) "Lone Strangers Strawberry Patched" (novel excerpt); and *Story Harvest* (2020) "Star-Spangled Go-Kart".

A non-fiction book for parents, *Nature's Ritalin for the Marathon Mind*, was published by Upper Access.

PRAIRIE WARBLER
©2021 by R. L. Mullins, Jr.

Zee-zee-zee. Zee-zee-zee.

Rachel was taking comfort in the nature sounds. The somewhat unkempt farm, with its stands of cedar and brushy areas, was perfect habitat for the Prairie Warbler. With its gold and black markings, like a proud Purdue Boilermaker, the bird brightens up a dreary scene while its song lifts many a spirit on a brisk Southern Indiana spring morning. That's why she hated to tidy up areas close to the old farmhouse for fear that she would lose the tiny chorus of warblers that wove their songs into her mornings through the open first floor windows.

Rachel tugged her sweater tighter to ward off the spring chill while listening to the tiny songsters and continued to sweep the old-fashioned way with a corn tassel broom she made herself. After dumping the dustpan, she felt that something was awry. Looking over the room, everything seemed in place. She heard hail striking her out-buildings, but that wasn't it. What? Her chorus! Where was her chorus?

Looking out the kitchen window, a giant funnel cloud against a grayish-green sky was coming. This was Mother Nature at her most unforgiving. It was both majestic and terrifying. The warblers were a lot smarter than she was. They must have sensed the pressure changes or whatever else they noticed and knew when to get out of town. She might not be that lucky. What did they say about windows? Open or shut? Rachel decided it didn't matter. If that thing wanted in her house, it was coming in. Southern Indiana was no stranger to tornadoes. Not much time to get to her root cellar refuge.

Looking around, Rachel grabbed her purse and a locket with a picture of Grant on their wedding day and made for the root cellar around back. The wind was picking up as she descended the porch stairs and slipped the last two steps. Her panic, like the wind, was starting to rise. In just those few moments it was blowing much harder and making it difficult to lift the wooden cellar door. If she lived through this, she was going to thoroughly oil those hinges. A moment that seemed to be a lifetime later, she got in, put the crossbar in place to hold the doors, and settled on the hard, pressure-treated wooden bench that Grant had built for them, away from the doors. Why did she grab the purse? That thing was useless down here, but her mother always said to take it everywhere you go. Thanks, Mom.

Grant had retrofitted this old hole in the ground to preserve their fruits and vegetables. He also put in electricity, some emergency supplies, and stores of bottled water and dried foods in case they were visited by a storm like this. Sitting there, she heard the old house creaking above and it sounded like a train was bearing down on it, but there were no railroad tracks in the area. The tornado was trying to suck the cellar doors off their hinges. Mother Nature, it seemed, sent Rachel's heart racing with an adrenalin spike that was both frightening and exhilarating. Her pulse felt like she was sprinting but there was no finish line—no end in sight.

She'd always thought that if she was ever in this situation, Grant would wrap her in a big hug and whisper that everything was going to be all right. Not anymore. Not since that horrible winter evening last year. She had called in the missing person report when he failed to come home. The accident report was pretty antiseptic. His pickup truck hit a slick spot on the winding Washington County road, lost control, bull-dozed the concrete parapet on the undersized one-lane bridge and did a flip into the Blue River. Grant was still strapped into his seat when they finally found him. Blunt force trauma. He was dead before he could drown. They knew this because there wasn't any water in his lungs. When the sheriff knocked on the door, a part of her died but there were so many good memories all around her. Rachel felt his comforting presence every single day.

Clicking open the locket with a photo of Grant in the black tuxedo that he had not wanted to wear, she said, "Wish you were here, babe. I miss you so much." Trying to lighten her mood, she remarked, "You're a little overdressed for this event, you know."

She clutched the locket to her breast and said a little prayer. The wind intensified for a few nerve-wracking moments, the lights winked out, and darkness reigned in the little hole as she squeezed the locket even tighter. Was this what it was like to be buried alive? The creaking of the wood frame house rose to a shriek and then...there was nothing. Silence. Rachel waited. She wasn't sure how long she sat in the darkness, but she talked to Grant through the whole thing. Just a quiet one-sided conversation, thank goodness, but it gave her a hint of peace to feel that he was right there beside her.

Finding a flashlight, she stood and said, "Okay, Grant. Ready to go see what's left of our little home?"

Unlocking the cellar door, she pushed hard but the thing just wouldn't budge. Looking through the tiny gaps in the boards, it appeared that the wheelbarrow had gotten lodged on top. Is that supposed to teach me to put my tools away?

"I want to see you again, sweetie, but I'm not going to die in this hole today to do it. Need your help, Grant. Push with me?"

It took all of her 125 pounds and a good deal of grunting to push the door and wheelbarrow up, but she finally did it. Surveying the area, the damage didn't seem too bad. Some shingles were missing from the barn and house. Those could be replaced pretty quickly. A bit of siding from the back of the house had been peeled off. It appeared that leaving the windows open didn't hurt the outside. No telling what the inside of the house looked like. A couple of the taller trees, including one big Chinese elm, were uprooted but they didn't damage anything other than a section of boundary fence. One electric pole was snapped, but the lines weren't sparking. The weathervane was missing. She'd look and, if necessary, contact the neighbors to see if one of them had found it. Finally, while not known for being the most wind-resistant of trees, the small cedars looked to be intact in her little warbler habitat. Hugging the locket to her again, she said, "Thanks for staying with me, sweetie. It looks like we made it out together. You always said you'd be here for me."

Zee-zee-zee. Zee-zee-zee.

"Thanks for the serenade, too."

About the author:

Rob Mullins writes from Prospect, Kentucky. He is an MFA candidate in Fiction at Spalding University. Rob is currently exploring characters under stress coming back from loss. He has co-authored a book on public policy as well as several journal articles on a variety of engineering and urban planning topics. Please look for more from him soon.

BREATHLESS
©2021 by Ronna L. Edelstein

In B.C.—the Before COVID world—Vera always woke up before her alarm, set for 6 a.m., rang; by the time she was ready to teach at 9 a.m., she had often done laundry, dashed to the grocery store for a few necessities, and dusted at least one room of her apartment. If she later napped, which she rarely did, it was always a brief respite to get a second wind. When she finally retired for the night—usually at 9 p.m., with time set aside for reading—she slept well, confident that she had led a productive, rewarding day.

Since March 14, 2020, the day she began self-isolating, Vera's energy level had depleted. The less she had to do, the more fatigued she felt. Her alarm jolted her awake at 8 a.m.; by 10:30 a.m., she was lying on the couch, eager for her first nap of the day. She did ride her stationary bike on a daily basis, but because she set it at a tension of zero, it did not demand a lot of physical output; she just rode in circles, a reflection of her life that had stopped moving forward. Two or three more naps left her tossing and turning at night; Vera woke up in the morning feeling physically exhausted.

But it was the mental fatigue that really plagued her. With no job—budget reductions due to the virus had caused her to lose her position as a writing teacher for university students—her mind seemed to have stagnated. Reading did exercise her mental muscle, but she could only read for a finite period of time before her eyes betrayed her. Because of her lack of external stimuli, Vera looked inward—focusing on the negatives caused by COVID-19: unemployment of her adult children and her; the closing of the theaters that nurtured her; the inability to hug another person and feel the warmth of their touch.

And now, Vera was struggling to find the energy to breathe. Anxiety had caused her breathing to turn shallow, making her feel as if she were in the midst of a 24/7 panic attack—or on the brink of a fatal heart attack. Vera spent her days trying to catch her breath, usually by yawning over and over again to bring in air. Not only did the yawning intensify her chronic jaw and head pain, but it also tired her. It took a lot of effort to breathe.

Fatigue from the "new normal" was aging Vera, stealing from her the *joie de vivre* and energy she once had. She felt broken—and breathless. With the present situation suffocating her and the future looking bleak, all Vera could do was turn to the past for the solace—and air—that she desperately sought.

From her position on the couch, Vera had a good view of part of the kitchen, all of the dining room, and most of the living room that made up her two-bedroom co-op. Although she lay under a thin blanket like a woman frozen in time, her eyes constantly moved from one room to the other, trying to find something to distract her from her faulty breathing and ongoing anxiety. On many days, her eyes seemed to gravitate to the dining room and its table, chairs, and china cabinet. The set, purchased in 1947—the year of Vera's birth—was, like Vera herself, beginning to show its age: nicks and scratches that resembled the thick veins and old age spots marring Vera's skin; discoloration of the blonde wood—reminding Vera of how gray hair was slowly replacing her once brunette strands; and seats that, despite numerous re-paddings, felt like concrete slabs. Yet, even the thought of getting rid of the dining room set had caused her tremors of separation anxiety—and had made it as hard to breathe then as it was now.

For Vera, the dining room set was more than wood and glass, nuts and bolts. It was her diary; it held memories of her beloved grandmother and parents and of her growing-up years; it was her personal storyteller that never ran out of tales to share. In a life of moves, transient friendships, and divorce, the dining room set provided Vera with a constant in a sea of change.

Before Ma stopped baking and retired the brown, hive-shaped cookie jar to the top of the china cabinet, it had held a place of prominence on the kitchen counter, glowing as if made of dark, thick honey. Even after countless washings and years of emptiness, the jar still permeated the dining room with the sweet aroma of Ma's home-baked Toll House chocolate chip cookies. Vera comprehended that the cookie jar could find a home in a new china cabinet or buffet, but it would just not be right.

Vera also refused to displace Ma's china dishes, which always had dominated the shelves of the china closet. With their decorative branches of blues and grays, the dishes created a peaceful autumnal scene—one that calmed Vera and eased her breathing. Every time Ma used those dishes, Dad had told the story behind their acquisition. Shortly after Vera's parents had married in 1939, Grandma had had a strange dream—one which she only shared with one of her steady customers in the grocery store owned by her stepson. The customer translated the facts of the dream into numbers, Grandma played those numbers, and her sole gambling venture won her the money to buy the dishes as a belated wedding gift for her son and new daughter-in-law.

It would be wrong to move the wine decanter and glasses that shared space with the dishes. Those Venetian glass pieces, with their nuances of yellow and bright brown, shone like the waters of Capri shimmering under a golden sun. Vera had bought the glassware for Grandma when traveling in Italy, but her parents had inherited the set after Grandma died. Maybe, Vera used to think, her son and daughter would raise those glasses in a toast to her—and to the family who had loved them.

Behind the sliding doors at the bottom of the china cabinet sat a wooden chest that held its own special treasure—a service for twenty-four of Coronation silverware. Dad had bought the silverware for Ma during the early years of their marriage. Whenever Vera polished the pieces with Ma, she reveled in Ma's reminisces about dinner parties and Mah-jongg gatherings that featured the silverware.

The table had stories to tell, too. Vera must have been about five years old when she rushed to the door to greet Dad upon his return from work. In her youthful exuberance, she ran into him and knocked out her loose front tooth. The next thing she knew, Dad had picked her up and laid her on the dining room table. The lights in the chandelier danced like pieces of fairy dust as Dad held her hand and Ma placed ice against her sore gums. The next morning, Vera had awakened to a gift from the Tooth Fairy hidden under her pillow.

That same dining room table had later turned into a Jackson Pollock canvas of orange splatters when Vera's older brother decided to shake a full bottle of orange soda to see what would happen when he opened it. One special time the table became the setting of a dinner party attended only by Ma and Vera. They spent hours talking about everything—from the days of Ma's youth to Vera's dreams of going to graduate school to become a teacher.

Vera knew she was being silly about not updating the dining room set, but whenever she set the table, enjoyed a meal, or dusted the furniture, she felt anchored. This table was where Grandma had taught Vera's son to play gin rummy and where she had entertained Vera's daughter by making dolls from tissues. Whenever Vera cleaned the glass of the china cabinet, she pictured Ma—dressed in a sleeveless shirt, pedal pushers, and a hairnet—rubbing that glass until it gleamed.

Although Vera understood that objects broke and rusted and that furniture wore out, she still needed that dining room set as much as she need the stuffed monkey her parents had given her after a childhood tonsillectomy. Vera liked being able to touch her past in a tangible way.

Memories of the dining room set had made Vera temporarily forget about her aloneness and loneliness as a quarantined 73-year-old. It had distracted her from her breathing challenges, but her yawning returned just as Vera mentally returned from the past to the present. Once again, she found herself breathless, wondering if she should call 911 and risk going to a pandemic-infested emergency room or remain on the couch and find another memory to sustain her. She chose to lay immobile, again letting her eyes take her from the unfriendly present to a more welcoming past.

The theatre posters that hung throughout the living room, reminders of the many adventures she and her children had shared on Broadway and in more local cultural venues, captured her attention. Vera had always known she could not dance, sing, or act. Her parents, in an effort to give her some creative outlet, had signed her up for violin lessons when she was six or seven, but every tune she played sounded like a chalk-on-the blackboard version of "Twinkle, Twinkle, Little Star." Vera had no artistic talent, but she did have a soul that yearned for the smell of the greasepaint and the roar of the crowd. She fed that soul by taking trips to Manhattan and buying season tickets to local theatres; for the past seventeen years, she had served as an usher at several theatres in her city's Cultural District. As an usher, she focused on the comfort of her patrons; erratic breathing never became an issue. As an usher, she discovered a sub-population of men and women who shared her passion for musicals, dramas, and comedies.

Vera had loved dressing in her white shirt, black pants, black socks, and black shoes. Sometimes she added a jacket to the ensemble; one theatre even requested that she wear a vest and bow tie. Although she sometimes felt like a waitress marching off to work or a penguin waddling across the ice, once Vera entered the theatre, where the guards nodded in recognition or the lobby chandelier shone on her like a spotlight, she knew she was where she belonged.

Vera did not mind stuffing programs before the show or cleaning up the programs and other debris left behind by patrons once the show had ended. She did not resent having to smile at patrons who pushed their way to the front of the line or refused to stand to allow other patrons to easily get to their seats. For Vera, ushering was worth any of the negatives it had because it allowed her—a talentless nobody—to be a part of the magic of theater. She got to seat dozens of tiny Belles dressed in glittering golden gowns, knowing they would be awed by the production of "Beauty and the Beast." She got to see little boys who would normally spend their weekends on the baseball field cheering for "Honus and Me," a play about the sport they loved. For Vera, life as an usher was a cabaret—one of excitement and fulfillment.

Then, the curtain closed and the lights went dark, leaving Vera to exchange her ushering clothes for a T-shirt and pajama bottoms. The theatre that had left her breathless with joy and wonder was gone; now despair and fear caused her a different kind of breathlessness.

Vera scanned the room, seeking something else to distract her from the heaviness in her chest—from the concern that the next breath would be her last. The Green Lady seemed to understand Vera's angst for she smiled at Vera from her perch upon the round glass table in the corner of the living room. Although the Green Lady, a porcelain figurine standing a foot tall, had traveled with Vera throughout her life—from her childhood home to her current residence—Vera had no knowledge of the Green Lady's origins. She did not know if Ma and Dad had purchased her or received her as a gift, but she did know that they had valued her. "Be careful, Vera! Don't knock down the Green Lady when you dust her!" Ma had warned Vera. "Make sure you avoid the Green Lady while practicing the forward roll on the living room floor," Dad had admonished. Only the Green Lady, with her Mona Lisa smile and green hair that seemed to fall in waves down her back, appeared unconcerned about her safety.

The artificial flowers in the baskets held in each of the Green Lady's hands looked real to Vera. She rose from the couch and gingerly leaned over the flowers to inhale their fragrance. Although a musty odor reached her nostrils—a thin layer of dust covered the paper-thin petals—Vera imagined she was sauntering in a garden and had stopped to admire the Eden-like beauty of the flora and fauna. In Vera's mind, the faux flowers exuded the aroma of Grandma's freshly baked apple pie, of Dad's after-shave lotion, of Ma's gardenia-like cologne. COVID and breathlessness dissipated as Vera lost herself in the Green Lady's love and serenity. She took a deep breath, relishing the sense of freedom that accompanied the easy inhaling and exhaling of air.

Yet, even though the past was real and comforting to Vera and the present was alien and fragile, Vera knew she could not live in the past. She knew that memories could only sustain her for a finite time; eventually, she would have to deal with the uncertain, complicated present and the even more frightening future—one that loomed like an endless, empty field with no sign of life. She would have to figure out how to survive days without social contact, nights when dreams of ventilators disturbed her sleep, weeks when she wished time to speed up, and months when she wanted time to slow down. She would have to figure out how to move forward when her feet turned backward and every part of her desired to return to a more secure past where COVID was not a part of the cultural lexicon.

Vera returned to the couch and turned on the television. While watching some mindless reality show would perhaps distract her from her stress, Vera instead chose to torment herself by watching the 24/7 international news station. "COVID resurgence in different nations." "Death toll from COVID soars above 225,000 in the United States." "Politicians extending quarantine, social distancing, and mask wearing."

She clasped her hands over her ears to silence the devastating words of the reporters. She closed her eyes to not read the closed captioning that scrolled across the bottom of her television screen. But no matter what Vera did, she could not escape the present—a repeat of yesterday and a foreshadowing of tomorrow. The A.C.— After COVID world—loomed like a dream always beyond Vera's reach; she feared she would not live to welcome it—or enjoy its rewards.

Lying on the couch, viewing the current world through a dark lens, Vera yawned and yawned and yawned until she gagged. She was an aging woman struggling in a world that took her breath away.

About the author:

Ronna Lynn Edelstein is a mother, avid reader, active theatregoer, and lifelong learner and teacher. She tries to find meaning and beauty in the world around her—and in those who inhabit it. Her work, both fiction and non-fiction, has appeared in the following: *Dream Quest One* (first place), *First Line Anthology, Pulse: Voices from the Heart of Medicine, SLAB: Sound and Literary Artbook, Quality Women's Fiction, Ghoti Online Literary Magazine,* and the *Pittsburgh Post-Gazette* and *Washington Post,* among others. Ronna thanks Scribes Valley for publishing "Breathless," her thirteenth story starring Vera.

BUS RIDE
©2021 by Leslie Muzingo

"I've changed my mind—I don't want to go!" Vanessa cried. She widened her stance and grabbed the door frame to prevent being forced into the car. But her nephew, Darnell, had anticipated her, and he gave her a hefty push before she got a good hold.

Vanessa fell face first onto the back seat. She felt her dress hike up her fat legs, but before she could think of anything but her embarrassment, her nephew had lifted her legs and turned them so that her entire body was in the back seat. Darnell threw her purse next to her. The door slammed shut, the locks clicked, and before she could protest, Darnell was driving them away.

Once oriented, Vanessa shot up and smacked Darnell upside his head. "I told you I didn't want to go to your damn ceremony!"

Darnell grinned at his aunt through the rear-view mirror while he drove. "Did you? I recall you telling me you'd be proud to come listen to the first black valedictorian at Shaw High give his speech."

"You must've drugged me if you got me to say that."

Darnell laughed. "I didn't drug you, and you *did* say it. Only family will be there, so you can calm down. I've got you a mask if you don't have one in your purse. Now sit back and enjoy the ride."

Vanessa sat back, but she couldn't calm down. The turmoil of the past churned inside her. She looked out the window and saw an empty school bus pass by. That image was enough to trigger events she had tried to suppress for almost forty years.

Momma had preached the same thing every day at the breakfast table before I left for school—"Be careful, stay safe, keep your mouth shut, don't talk back, avoid empty rooms and corners"—and I was sick of hearing it. Without thinking about the pop in the mouth I'd earn for back-talking, I slammed my spoon to the table and cried, "Momma, I've had enough! I have friends at that school! Friends! White friends! No one there is going to hurt me. Me and the other eleven black kids have ridden that bus all year. Nothing has happened yet, so please stop it."

Momma stood there holding her pregnant belly in her hands, listening but not speaking. For a full minute, the kitchen was quiet except for the sound of the ticking clock and the mockingbird and blue jay fighting for territory outside. Finally, Momma spoke. "The key word in what you said, Missy, is *yet*. Nothing has happened *yet*. But don't expect your joy to last. You need to prepare for change."

"Oh, Momma, don't be so—"

A hand flew in the air and hit me square in the mouth. "Don't be so what? You need to keep your mouth shut and your ears open, daughter. You don't pay attention to squat if you think nothing has happened. A young man being hung on a tree, dying, is nothing, I suppose."

"Dying?" I wanted to press my hand against my mouth to soothe it like a bandage, but I knew better. Momma wanted to see me strong and mindful. I sat up straight and looked into her eyes so she'd know I was listening.

Although her words that immediately followed were harsh, she gave me a nod of approval before she spoke. "You heard me. A young man, Michael Donald, was found dead last week, hanging from a tree outside'a his momma's home—"

"Michael Donald! I know him!"

"Lotsa folks knew him. Everyone called him a hardworking, honest young man. Someone saw it happen, but a'course he can't tell the police. It hasn't even made the papers. Not yet. But it will."

Tears stung my eyes and streamed down my cheeks. I tried to stop them, but they were like time, unstoppable. Momma despised weakness, so I turned my head away so she couldn't see my face.

But Momma jerked my head back and held my chin to make me face her.

"Don't you turn away from me! You need to listen to this! You think those white children are your friends. Maybe they are. But some of them have nasty parents who have bad hearts like the people who killed Michael. And bad parents teach their children to be bad."

Tears flooded my face as I jerked my head away. "But not all of them are bad! Not all! I know they were bad when you were a girl, but not anymore! So, until you have more proof, leave it alone!"

Momma backed away and looked at me for a moment. When she spoke, her voice was firm, but soft. "You need to get to the bus stop or you'll miss school."

I grabbed my books and headed for the door.

"But before you go, know this: two days ago, a noose was hanging from the flagpole at Davidson High School. The black kids being bussed there thought the white kids were their friends too." She left the room before I could say a word.

I was quiet on the bus. I wanted privacy so I could think about all Momma had said. Michael Donald, dead? He was such a nice boy, almost a man. I had been hoping he'd ask me out. I wanted to cry loud enough for Michael in heaven to hear me, but of course, this was not the place. I promised myself I'd grieve for Michael later. The noose hung at Davidson High confused me. I didn't get it. Surely no one planned to string up any of the kids on the bus.

My private thoughts didn't last long. Little John, a senior boy who stood almost seven feet tall, was in one of his moods, and he wasn't leaving anyone alone. He wanted to sing the song he'd made up.

"Nessa! You'll sing 'Segregation Bus' with me, won't you? Not whisper-sing this time, let's let the driver hear us, okay?"

I had no intention of singing, not on that day. But I could tell Little John was in a mood, and I felt that I should prevent trouble if I could. "Come sit with me, Little John. Tell me how you came to make up that song."

Little John kneeled on the seat in front of me. "Can't sit next to you, don't you know that? My knees bang up against the seats. Course, I could sit in the front seat, but I'm not doing that. Not with ya'll sitting back here. So, you wanna sing my song?"

I smiled my prettiest at him. "How did you think of that song? And why did you put it to the tune of 'Multiplication Rock'?"

He looked me over a bit, then his eyes narrowed, and he spoke quieter and more deliberate, like my Momma does when she's trying to make sure I hear her. "I put it to that tune cuz we all grew up with it. And it is a school-type song. Just made sense." He stood up and looked hard at me. "*Why* I wrote it, you know, and everyone else here knows. Because they say we are being integrated, but they don't put anyone on this bus but us. They could pick someone else up on the way, but no, they want us segregated. And you're just asking me this because you're trying to keep me talkin' till we get to the school. You a purty girl, Nessa, but you ain't acting so purty. You better wise up, cuz things are coming down, and we need to be ready to fight. But not now. Right now, I'm gonna sing."

Little John straightened up tall before he burst forth into his song. I looked around the bus and saw that nobody was paying us any attention. They kept themselves busy looking out the windows, into a book, or down at the floor.

Shandra, my best friend, sat behind me, so I whispered to her, "What's going on?"

"Friend-girl, don't you know?"

"I know about Michael Donald if that is what you mean."

Shandra's braids snapped back and forth as she shook her head.

"Then you mean about what happened at Davidson?" I was looking up front to see if the half-deaf bus driver had heard Little John over the noise of the old bus.

Again, Shandra shook her head, only this time her braids were closer to the bus window and slapped against the glass.

"Then, what?"

Shandra leaned forward. "You don't have no baby brother or sisters yet, not till your momma has the baby. That's why you didn't hear. But what everyone is freaking out about is that some white man is trying to get the kids from Booker T. Elementary into his car."

"What!"

"The Principal from over there sent home a note last night to all the parents telling them about it. He said they shouldn't worry, but that he thought they should know."

Gemmy, a girl who always knew what was happening, slid in Shandra's seat. "I heard you talking about what happened at Booker T."

Shandra didn't really like Gemmy. I knew that for a fact. She turned to her and said, "Now how do you know what I said? I was whispering, and this bus is loud."

Gemmy didn't bat an eye. "I read your lips. Anyway, just wanted to tell you it didn't just happen at Booker T. Someone's trying to pick up the kids at Bessie Fondren school too."

"Segregation Bus! Segregation Bus!" sang out Little John at the top of his lungs. He clapped his hands to the tune.

"What's going on back there!" the bus driver half-hollered.

Darius, a boy Shandra had a crush on, got out of his seat and strode over to Little John. I couldn't hear what they said, but it was obvious from the boys' faces that Darius was trying to calm Little John down and that Little John didn't appreciate Darius' opinion one bit.

Shandra leaned forward and whispered in my ear, "Are they gonna fight? I don't want them to fight. Little John is a lot bigger than Darius. He might hurt Darius."

I was about to say no, there wouldn't be a fight because we were almost to school when Little John cried out, "Those white bastards!" He ran to the door, and the bus hadn't even stopped yet. Darius ran right behind him, and the other boys all fell in behind.

The bus stopped, and the driver opened the door. It wasn't till then that I could see what made our guys run like hell 'a fire out the door and across the front lawn of our school. They were mad enough to kill. Mad enough to kill whoever hung the nooses at our school.

There wasn't just one noose hanging from the flagpole like they had at Davidson High. Shaw High had nooses hanging from the flagpole, from the school windows, and even from the four front columns. There were twelve nooses, one for each of us on the bus.

Without saying a word to us girls, the bus driver got off the bus and pushed in the lock. We were trapped. We couldn't run and couldn't help.

Little John, Darius, and the other boys were yelling on the school's front lawn. I guess they were yelling. The driver parked our bus far enough away from the front of the school and the windows of the bus were all up, so I couldn't hear anything. But I could see their mouths opening wide and their arms hitting the air.

A couple of the guys started taking the nooses down off the columns in front of the school. That's when the white boys came out of the front door of the school. I knew all of them—big, strong boys who played on the basketball and football teams. There were twelve white guys to our six, and they walked out onto that lawn as if they owned it. But these were Little John's friends. He played sports with these fellas. Everything was going to be fine.

The rest of the girls must've felt the same because for a moment the tension that had been in the air had disappeared. We looked at each other with bright eyes. Shandra even smiled.

Gemmy's scream tore through the bus and almost ripped it in two. My head jerked up, and I looked in time to see Little John's face bloodied by two guys I thought were his friends. One guy held his arms while the other threw hard punches first to his face, then to his gut. Darius was trying to talk to the white boys, but they laughed at him and beat him, too. All of our boys had two white boys beating them. They didn't have a chance.

We girls were a collective of silent fear. We didn't know what would happen next to the boys or to us. I thought of Momma and all she said about white people, and Michael Donald, and I silently cried. I wanted my momma there, to protect me and to tell me what to do. I didn't know what would happen next, none of us did, and the fear gripped me by the throat, leaving me helpless. All I could do is pray, "Oh Lord, Lord, Lord, please help us, please help our boys, please help me, I am so afraid!"

Little John, Darius, and the rest of the boys were all on the ground. But I fixed my eyes on this one boy, Arthur, who I hardly knew. He was a freshman, and small for his age. Why did it seem he bled more? They were all far away from us, yet close enough that I could see them all clearly. But Arthur, my view of him was different. Why did he seem to pop out from the rest? He was so clean cut and quiet. Maybe he seemed like a sacrificial lamb. Maybe he reminded me of Michael Donald, a boy in the wrong place at the wrong time. Maybe I just wanted to take him in my arms, hold him, and take his tears on my breast, cry upon his injured head, and ask Jesus why oh why did this happen?

Those white boys who we thought were Little John's friends took our boys by the wrists and dragged them away. All except Arthur. Arthurs arms were so short that the white guys assigned to him had to bend over to drag him. They tried doing that, and some kids hollered at them from the school windows, so they gave up moving him that way. They talked between themselves. Then one pushed the other, that one pushed back, till the first one shrugged and picked up little ole Arthur and slung him up over his shoulder like he was a sack of grain. I could see that other guy laughed, but the one carrying Arthur was busy catching up to the other fellas. Soon they all disappeared from sight.

One of the school cafeteria workers came out to dump some trash. He was a friendly guy and always joked with us girls. Today he kept his head down and walked silently past our bus. Was he scared too? Or did he know the plans for us and didn't want to get involved? I had a hard lump in my throat after he went back to the kitchen without a glance our way.

We girls sat on that bus for three more hours. It got hot as an oven, but none of us opened a window. I guess we were all scared that someone would do the impossible and squeeze through a window if we opened them, or throw something inside, or something even worse that we hadn't thought of yet. The unknown was worse than what we had seen, and what we had seen was worse than what we'd ever imagined could happen with integration. Now we all knew about the man going by the elementary schools trying to get kids in his car, we all knew about Michael Donald, and we all knew that bad things didn't just happen to someone else, and we were so damned scared we could hardly breathe. The sound of my heart beating was so loud that it made it hard to pray, I could only think, *Oh Lord Jesus, please forgive me for anything bad I've ever done, I want you to take me to heaven if I'm about to die, but please, Jesus, I'm young and I want to live!*

The sun was high in the sky and beating down on the bus when those white boys showed up again. This time they dragged our guys between 'em, one holding each arm, and they were lifting them up more kind of like they were displaying them to the world. With Arthur being so small, they held him the highest.

They dragged our guys to the bus and stood there and waited for what we didn't know. Some guys began making obscene gestures at us. The other girls began making noises like they thought those guys planned to rape us or something, but my mind flew to other conclusions. "Girls!" I hissed. "Think! They wouldn't be bringing the boys back if they planned to rape us! They wouldn't be raping us in front of the bus driver! Just settle down and wait. Nothing we can do no how. But stay calm and keep your minds sharp."

Everyone became silent once more. We didn't look at the boys; we looked straight ahead and waited for what we didn't know. It wasn't long after that the bus driver and the school principal showed up. The bus driver unlocked the door and got in his seat. Then the white boys came on the bus and dropped our guys in the front seats. Once they left, the Principal came on the bus.

He walked straight to the back. His words were friendly, but his eyes were mean as hell. "I'm going to give you ladies the rest of the day off. Make sure these ruffians get home. Tell their parents about the fight they started. You understand?"

"But—" Gemmy began.

I gave her a sharp look, which shut her up.

"You got something to say, girl?" the principal asked.

"No sir," Gemmy replied.

"What about you, Vanessa?"

I kept my eyes on the floor. "No, sir."

Without another word, the principal walked off the bus. The bus driver started the engine, and the bus inched away, but then someone banged on the door. The driver stopped the bus, opened the door, and in ran one of the biggest of those white boys who'd beat up our fellas. He was carrying a noose. He ran straight to me.

"Give this to Little John when he wakes up." He threw the noose in my lap and ran off the bus.

After that, we black girls hung out together at school. No white friends for any of us. When you can't tell your friends from your enemies, it is best to stick with what you know is true.

I graduated from Shaw High School a year later. I've never gone back.

The day had warmed by the time they got to Shaw High School, but it was still pleasant for May in Mobile. A podium and two chairs sat before a semi-circle of eight chairs on the right-center of the school's lawn. Vanessa shook when she walked to her seat, but family members took her arms and supported her.

"We're here for you as much as Darnell," her sister Geneva whispered.

"Oh, that's not true," Vanessa replied, but it still made her feel comforted to know her family understood her fear.

"Sure it is. And I think those folks behind you are here for you, and Michael Donald, and all the kids that rode your bus."

Vanessa turned around and saw that people had gathered across the road from the school. Everyone wore masks, and they all stood at least six feet apart. Some stood on their cars. Others had crossed the road and stood by the school columns, probably hoping to get a better view. It hit Vanessa that a few must have been Darnell's classmates because they were Darnell's age and wore the traditional cap and gown in the Shaw High School colors. They waved at Darnell, and he waved back.

The family sat in the semi-circle of seats while the principal and Darnell sat in the two seats behind the podium. The principal stood and approached the podium. "I'm glad I thought to hook up a microphone!" Laughter came rolling in from behind Darnell's family, and the principal grinned. "Get your phones ready to record the only graduation ceremony for 2020 held in Mobile!" The principal paused, and then said, "I'm so glad Darnell's family accepted this invitation to his ceremony, and I'm happy I could offer it. Thank you for all wearing masks. It is by following the COVID-19 rules I can show the School Board that this event was a success and, heaven help us, if we still must resort to this type of ceremony next year, the Board will allow it to happen again. I always want to have a ceremony for all of our graduates, but that was impossible this year. By the way, it is great seeing so many of our current graduates out there in the cheap seats!

Laughter and cheers came from across the road. Some of the students even waved their graduation caps. After they settled down, the principal continued.

"Hopefully, we won't have to do a small service like this next year. But I had no trouble getting the Board to agree this time because the student in question was Darnell.

"Darnell, as all of you know, is extremely special. Yes, he is the first black valedictorian from our school. But more than that, he was an inspiration to all the students here at Shaw. He wasn't merely the smartest student, but he was also the kindest and the bravest. One day I brought him into my office. I had to know what motivated him to be the person he had grown up to be. I expected him to tell me about his mother, which of course he did. But then he told me about his aunt, who had been one of the integrated students here at Shaw. I don't want to take away from Darnell's shining moment but let me just say for those of you who don't know about it, that in 1981 an incident occurred here that is a shameful part of Mobile's history. A week after Klan members hung Michael Donald, someone, probably students, displayed twelve nooses here on this lawn. The six black boys who attended school here as part of integration, leaped from the bus they rode and protested the action. In response, twelve white students came out and beat those six boys unconscious. While all this was happening, the six black girls bussed here with those boys, one of which was Darnell's aunt, sat on that bus, locked in by the driver, for over three hours. They watched their friends beaten and drug away. They sat in fear, not knowing what was going to happen to them. What a thing for a high school girl to go through. Yet it showed me where Darnell got his strength."

Darnell's mother, Geneva, leaned over and whispered in Vanessa's ear, "He's known about what happened to you for years. Heard it from some friend on the street, I spect."

"It has been glorious having Darnell as a student here at Shaw. I'll miss him. But maybe I'll get another child from this same strong and loving family before I retire. I sure hope so. Now, here's the Shaw High School valedictorian, Darnell Howard."

The Principal return to his seat, and Darnell stood and approached the podium. The applause from the uninvited guests stopped the boy. He put up his hand, but everyone only applauded louder. He opened his mouth to speak, and the applause was louder still. Darnell at last accepted his honor and bowed his head.

While Darnell stood with his head bowed, Vanessa turned around and looked at the crowd cheering behind them. There were more people gathered than before—even more than she could have imagined. She watched them for a brief moment. Then she turned and got comfortable so she could listen to her nephew's speech.

About the author:

Leslie Muzingo lives in Mobile, Alabama in winter and Fortune Cove, Prince Edward Island in the summer and fall when COVID allows her across the border. She has been a contest winner with *Two Sisters Writing and Publishing* five times, has been published in two of their anthologies, and expects to be published in their 2020 anthology this spring. She has been a finalist with Scribes Valley Publishing twice and published in their *Where Tales Grip* and *Beyond the Norm* anthologies. Other publications include stories in: *Darkhouse Books, Mother's Milk Books, Pink Panther Magazine, Curating Alexandria,* among others. She is working on a novel that takes place in Maritime Canada and Ireland.

THE PANDORA PANACEA
©2021 by John Baldwin

Being immortal is exhausting. Remaining always youthful and beautiful sounds wonderous, of course. But one must regularly change their life and identity to disguise the inexplicable lack of aging. And if that isn't curse enough, how about being the infamous person linked to the ending of the Golden Age of Man many thousands of years ago? That was a time when polytheism was the accepted belief. Her name has become a metaphor for that dreadful event—to mean something that is best left untouched. She is the living (well, forever living) truth of that tale. She goes by the name Dora in today's world. Her real name might be familiar to you: *Pandora*. Not so much born, as created—by the gods of Olympus.

In the year 2020, Dora's language skills and literary knowledge made her a shoo-in to work for a publishing company. One day she came across something of interest: a young man named Greg had submitted draft pages of a proposed humorous little book. The book would illustrate in simple line drawings common annoyances suffered by everyone: Stubbed toe; lettuce embarrassingly stuck in one's teeth; and the like. Dora had been assigned to meet him at the office to determine whether a finished work might seem worth publishing.

Upon meeting, Dora began. "Greg, it's a most clever book. Did you bring some additional pages for us to see?"

Gaining his composure after being shocked by her beauty, Greg said, "Er, yes. Here you are." He passed them over. "One is the embarrassment of walking into a sliding glass door. Then there's a splinter in the finger. Stepping on dog doo is another good icky subject. I thought the whimsical drawings matched up pretty well. Besides which," he added sheepishly, "it's the only art talent I possess."

Dora gave him credit. "Some of Picasso's best works were contour line drawings. The French artist Honoré Daumier used witty drawings as caricatures of absurdities." She caught herself from listing other examples from histories so familiar to her. "I believe your simple illustrations portray the unwelcome experiences perfectly."

They chatted for another half hour about some other examples he had in mind and the illustrations that might accompany them.

"Greg, I quite like your book," Dora said. "Mind you, I'll just be passing on my opinion. I must ask though: What motivated you to create this parade of human ouches?"

"I actually had a serious purpose in mind. It's just so distressing to me that people nowadays are so polarized. This was one small way I could show how much all of us, everywhere, truly have in common."

"That's a noble objective. Would you consider yourself a do-gooder?"

"Oh, most definitely. Most of my acquaintances think I'm hopelessly naïve. I simply believe that man is essentially good."

"That is a most refreshing perspective. But how about the existence of crime, poverty, greed...and all the other negative aspects of our society? How can you reconcile those with your humanitarian views?"

"I can't. I just have a sense that these unpleasant things were somehow imposed upon our natural state."

"Is that a Christian view? Maybe expecting the world to be purified upon the return of Jesus? Or some other religion's vision of a heavenly existence?"

"No, I'm not that kind of believer. I don't even accept the premise of just one god." Her expression of interest influenced him to continue. "If there is any Supreme Force, it seems to me that Polytheism—multiple gods—might provide a better explanation for our human circumstances than any of the alternatives. Anyway, my farfetched dream would be to overcome, or at least reduce, life's obstacles and somehow make this a better world now...in our lifetime. Oh, there I go, getting preachy with my outlier beliefs. You can see why people think I'm an idiot."

"No, Greg, I don't think that at all. The uncommon person who is down-deep honest and cares for others is always considered a fool and subject of ridicule. I think of the character Prince Mishkin in Dostoyevsky's *The Idiot,* and Billy Budd in Melville's tragic novel. They were admirable, if ill-fated, examples of how people could be truly good."

"Hey, you're talking my language as someone trained in classic literature. Hardly seems like the training for the creation of my silly book, does it?"

"I've had more careers myself than you could imagine."

"It is so refreshing to talk with you, though mostly I've done the talking. "

"I'll let you know about our company's interest in publishing your book. But I must ask. In your study of the classics, did you come across the poet Hesiod?"

"Sure, and his poems *Theogony* and *Works and Day,* from about the seventh century B.C. He wrote about the gods of Olympus and how they imposed miseries upon mankind. These spirits were mistakenly released from a box, or jar, as I recall. Even attempted to read these works in the original Greek."

Dora brightened. "Greg, you interest me greatly. We must meet again."

Stunned, Greg replied, "Dora, you overwhelm me. But why would you want to see me again? Frankly, you are definitely out of my league."

"Oh, Greg. Those things are so superficial. You might be the exact person I've been seeking for such a long...long...time."

"Summon Prometheus!" roared Zeus, "I want to be

entertained."

Zeus needn't have bellowed, but that seemed only fitting for the king of the gods dwelling on Olympus. The lesser gods made efforts to appease Zeus and his unpredictable urges. His displeasures could prove eternally painful.

Prometheus shortly appeared. "You asked for me, Your Highest. How might I serve you?"

"Prometheus, we defeated your giant Titans and you became a sort of humanoid god-man. I held no grudge for this until you dared to defy me centuries ago. After granting you the privilege of creating the first creatures to live on Earth, you dared to steal and hand over to them the gift of fire. For that transgression, I had you tortured horribly. As a further lasting punishment of humans for accepting the fire, I had fashioned the first in the race of women and a wife to your Brother Epimetheus. She was to be the subject of the cruelest of tricks to be played upon mankind."

"These punishments were deserved, My King. I am blessed by the return to your favor."

"Do recite for me again this amusing tale about the results of my sport. I've paid no attention since then to the earthly world's existence."

"As you wish. The woman so formed we named *Pandora*, meaning all-endowed, as each of the gods gave her certain gifts. Athena blew life into her; Aphrodite bestowed beauty and desire; Hermes, the gift of speech. Your ingenious trick was to incorporate into Pandora evil traits of deviousness, falsehood, and treachery that would prove to be a curse on her husband. Furthermore, as a dowry gift she was given a box, which she was instructed to never open."

Zeus beamed. "Yes, I recall well. Her inherent female curiosity caused her to open the box and...tell me this part again."

"Escaping from the container were the full range of evils that could plague humanity—hatred, envy, greed, disease, poverty, pain, war and death. The only positive left behind as a token to mankind was Hope. That has been the condition of the human world ever since."

Zeus laughed heartily. "A fitting condition for pitiful mortals. And what of Pandora after that calamity?"

"She was known to have been inconsolable with guilt for that event, though she had meant no harm. She did later have children with Epimetheus and the family eventually passed on as humans do...except Pandora, who lived on. Perhaps accidentally in her formation, she was given a few god-like qualities, including immortality. That's all I know. I haven't visited that world for ages."

"Well, perhaps you should. I realize you were once sympathetic and even lived among them for a while. My interest is merely that their pathetic little lives might provide some novel amusement for us."

"Dora, we've now been together lots of times these last few months. It has been exhilarating and, at times, exhausting. There has been time enough to know one another."

"Yes, Greg. It has shown me that your life is lived consistently with your scruples. I saw the effort you expended to calm the little lost girl in the shopping center. Then to reconnect the child with her mom. You crossed the busy street to assist a handicapped woman take groceries into her apartment. I've observed you telling the absolute truth when a slight lie would have benefitted you."

"Those are inconsequential little things."

Dora responded, "I know better. They portray the larger truths. I saw you take on personal risk to aid someone vulnerable. We saw two bullies harassing a homeless person and you intervened. Angry at the disruption, they were about to throw punches. It was a fight you would have lost. You showed bravery in a lost cause."

Greg responded honestly. "More like stupidity than bravery. But then you intervened. Coming face to face, you stopped them in their tracks with this: 'You rascally knaves. You base dunghill villains. You are proof of Lucius Seneca's quote: All cruelty springs from weakness.' You, Dora the dominator, delivered two perfectly placed kicks to the thighs of these thugs. They cried out in pain and dropped to their knees disabled. You dispatched the bullies like a seasoned street fighter, while quoting Shakespeare, and a first century Roman philosopher, I believe. Where did all that come from?"

"These were just things I learned over time. Some memorable quotes. Simple kicks to their sciatic nerves. You were the brave one. No doubt you'd have beaten them up as well."

"Not hardly. You know my personal history. My limitations. My aspirations, etc. And I know hardly anything about you. Except that you are remarkable in everything you do. I've seen that during the wondrous times we've had together."

"We've played different kinds of games. Visited galleries. Tried our hands at various sports."

"Enjoyable to be sure...but hardly competitive. You not only beat me almost every time, though very courteous about it, but had near perfect scores besides. We went to museums and you recounted historical details about every famous leader memorialized there and their cultures. As a lark, we went to an archery range. You were unfamiliar with the modern compound bow, yet still hit the bullseye repeatedly."

"You weren't so bad yourself at some activities." Flirtatiously, she continued, "Certainly, when we had private times together, you proved to be a most ardent lover."

"Oh, please. There could be no luckier fellow in this department. It was as if you brought to bear all the bedroom skills of celebrated women throughout the ages—Cleopatra, Madame Pompadour..."

"Don't forget the original Eve, or the goddess Athena, for that matter."

"Dora, I'm not kidding about that."

"Me, either. Greg, I've had to keep myself a mystery. If it's any comfort to you, no one living knows who I am, or where I came from. My special skills and broad knowledge *are* far from ordinary, that's true. There is a simple explanation, but one that you might find impossible to understand and accept."

"I'm ready to believe anything about you. My fascination and admiration for you, my mysterious lady, has become something much grander. I love you; that couldn't be a surprise to you. But every guy would. On top of everything else, you're a living Google, with knowledge of everything it seems. Cannot imagine why I've been blessed with the gift of you. I'll relish it while I can."

"Greg, I care for you as well. I've greatly enjoyed our many adventures. I'll confess though to having an ulterior motive in observing your behavior and responses to stimuli of different kinds. Are you familiar with the story of Diogenes from ancient Greece who carried a lantern in search of an honest person?"

"Well, sure. Was he supposed to have found one?"

"I happen to know that he did not. But *I* have. Our time together was my personal test to see if you are truly a genuinely honest, decent, moral person. You proved it. You are one of that elite group."

"Oh, come on. That makes me sound like...like Jesus Christ."

"I know the real him. Take away the son of God holiness later attributed to him and you do have the same values."

"Stop, that's too much. I'm just a regular guy, while you seem to be perfect in every way. Like a good witch, or a...a...goddess."

"I have my flaws, as you shall discover. I have come to trust you now completely and will reveal all. Let's find a bench in the park and you shall know me. You shall hear how Eve from the Garden of Eden and myself have something in common: We both transgressed against divine law and brought destruction to innocents."

"Thanks for accompanying me on this visit, Aphrodite. Zeus ordered me to revisit humankind. He still relished how he had succeeded in destroying the innocent all-male Paradise with unleashed suffering."

"Prometheus, I know all about it, though had no hand in its execution. The first earthly woman was created by him as a poisonous gift to your brother, Epimetheus. It was a punishment for your impudence, Prometheus, in giving humans the use of fire. Zeus has since forgiven you."

"Exactly. And the woman, Pandora, unable to resist temptation, opened the gifted box which released all the ugliness imaginable upon the Earth. Their population would have grown, but undoubtedly has continued to suffer terribly. It just occurred to Zeus that man's current struggles might provide good sport for the gods."

"As the goddess of love and beauty, observing the torment of humans would provide no pleasure to me. As someone once sympathetic to them, how do *you* feel about it?"

"I feel the same way but wouldn't dare provoke Zeus by any interference in his games."

"So, let's just observe how things are and report back to our King."

Seated on a park bench, Dora explained everything to an aghast Greg. "And that, my dear friend, is the story of why all people suffer in this world."

"You, lovely and perfect you, are the singular cause of all mankind's ills?"

"Yes, me. And I must correct your perception. I was created by the gods in Olympus and given some few of their abilities. I was not, however, made to be perfect. As explained, I was formed to be a woman who would tell lies and bring treachery, disobedience, and falsehood into men's lives. It has been only by force of will over centuries that I've been able to largely suppress these drives. But the eternal guilt remains for opening the box of horrors."

"Wow, that's a lot to swallow. At the core of what you're telling me is an acceptance that the Greek gods of Olympus are *the Higher Power!* It's a stretch, but I believe in you, so I can accept as true this creation history. After all, in ancient times these multiple gods *were* the religion. So, do they continue to be an active force in our lives?"

"No, Greg, I don't believe so. I lived through the ancient period when most people prayed to this group of gods. That has given way to a belief in monotheism—just one god—though it can be a somewhat different one for the major religions. Up in Olympus, I know that they've forgotten this earthly experiment for thousands of years—ever since they inflicted me on mankind."

"Oh, Dora, what a burden of guilt to carry for any person. But then, forgive my confusion, are you a human, or what?"

"I am almost entirely human, you could say, with some extra features built in. Like, say immortality."

"So, I've been dating and cavorting with someone who is thousands of years old and wise? Talk about an age difference. A big question looms. Why would you waste time with me, demonstrably an average mortal?"

"Not average at all, as my test proved. As someone one hundred percent good and honest, you are exceptional. You uniquely are qualified to join me in a grand effort to make life better for everyone. I caused all the woes suffered by the people. I've been planning for ages to launch an effort to substantially relieve these troubles. To accomplish this, I had to find a purely honest partner. You're the one, Greg. Will you join me?"

"Body and soul. That is, if souls are still a thing. Let's make our world better."

Invisibly watching this exchange, Prometheus confided in Aphrodite, "It looks like we've reestablished connection with the world at an ideal time. Guilt ridden Pandora and her selected partner will try to ease the hardships she caused to humanity. I will secretly hope for this to succeed. At least it should provide some entertainment for Zeus and the other gods."

Aphrodite proposed, "Let's go visible down here and sit down for some earth food. That will be a refreshing change. I'd favor hanging around then to hear Pandora's action plan. Seeing how she and Greg work and play together is bound to be fun as well."

They found a restaurant and seemed oblivious to the

excitement it generated among the customers. The most exquisite beauty in the company of a hero-proportioned man. Better than any other possible Hollywood celebrity sighting.

"I've been shaping this idea for making the world a better place for a long time. I am no genius but rather a keen observer who has seen the suffering of mankind over centuries. Have watched societies thrive and wither. All of this is attributable to the ills I introduced. Except for death, the other curses such as hatred, envy, greed, and prejudice have been embedded in humans...in their very DNA, I suppose."

"This is what you propose we fix? That's an ambitious undertaking even for remarkable you."

"Indeed so. It's only possible with the participation of yourself and other uniquely honest and decent men and women that might be found. In human history, and still today, there are those leaders and ordinary citizens who have somehow overcome all the curses with which I once infected man. Some few of such people have ruled their nations wisely and well, whether formed as established democracies, or enlightened monarchies. The same minority of ordinary citizens have also lived honorable lives—treating all others with compassion."

"I have heard of such rulers and encountered such people. They come and go it would seem."

"Yes, but that's just the starting point. The First Step. What if all such morally exceptional persons could be identified? Plato envisioned the development of philosophers who would be morally and intellectually suited to govern. Suppose in choosing any leader—whether for President, or for the local school board—that ideal person could be unquestionably determined? Voters would know that such a person would be impartial, acting without self-interest, and seeking to do what's best for everyone. But leaders aside, regular citizens who proved to be morally exceptional like yourself would be the absolute best friends and neighbors. I've chosen to call all such special people the Optimized.

"Well, sure, but how could an Optimized person be definitely identified? Every politician—hell, everyone for that matter—would likely claim that they qualify."

"That's the Second Step of my project. I informally tested you, but in fact a sophisticated test has been developed which can clearly establish whether someone is Optimized. It uses the most advanced techniques to evaluate emotions and probe the recorded histories of the subjects. I commissioned the development of this test by the leading experts in their fields."

"What? How could you have arranged and afforded all this?"

"Think about it. Cumulative experience and financial opportunities over generations. Count in the resources left me by departed husbands and lovers, some quite wealthy. Oh, sorry. That last thing might upset you."

"Being jealous seems rather trivial considering what you're talking about."

Dora smiled. "Then there's the final Step Three. The identity of the Optimized ones will be known. It follows that the public would prefer voting for and associating with them. These leaders will use logic and reason in their domains. The citizens will have their freedom and the law will be enforced fairly. In daily lives, Optimized friends will be those who are absolutely supportive and trustworthy. So here is the anticipated great conversion: By the qualities of honesty and caring shown by the Optimized, other people will over time be influenced to minimize or subdue their undesirable instincts. This will inevitably and eventually lead to a better, kinder world."

"O.K. Sign me up. When do we start?"

"Immediately. We will be launching an international campaign to promote the Optimized test. Those who pass will be officially credentialed. So, let's get started my dear all-human friend."

"Now that's something unexpected!" exclaimed Prometheus. "Who could have guessed that my creation Pandora would be starting a kind of revolution down here?"

"It would appear that this first woman on earth has risen above her humble origin. Might this be considered a challenge to the gods?"

"Oh, I don't believe so. What do we care if humans can make their lives a little less miserable? It will certainly prove interesting to see if this grand plan might work."

"Yes, Prometheus, and it gives us an excuse to stay on this planet a while longer. I confess to enjoying the attention we're receiving from the people we encounter here. Even as the most beautiful female of all creation, this goddess enjoys the admiration. I never receive compliments anymore from our counterparts in Olympus."

"Oh, I suppose we can extend our visit to see how Pandora's project works out before reporting back to Zeus."

The worldwide project was launched with great and expensive fanfare. It was the subject of interest exceeding all other news. Millions of people opted to take the Test. A small percentage passed this successfully and were certified. Regular people were at first anxious to be in the company of Optimums. Office seekers at all different levels of government proudly proclaimed their Optimum status seeking to be elected over their opponents.

Pandora and Greg were elated. They seemed on the way to changing the world for the better. Now they just had to wait and watch as the Optimum drive for goodness expands and succeeds.

Now, what could possibly go wrong with this project? Short answer: The power of evil. People who did not qualify as Optimums were *envious*. Their feelings took the form of *hate* against the designated more moral people. Pandora, despite wishing to be anonymous, was outed as a founder, and faced *prejudice* as some kind of hostile outsider (if they only knew). Most businesses uniformly resisted the project because their officers seldom qualified as Optimums. Those business leaders who did qualify were resisted by *selfish* stockholders who did not want social concerns limiting corporate profits. Institutions with policies that were not based on some form of *discrimination* condemned the entire idea of Optimums.

After a while, the harsh reality had to be acknowledged by Dora and Greg. The Project was a monumental failure. Human nature, as accentuated by the curses from Pandora's box, had won out over altruistic efforts to dilute these ills. Those people who had been certified as Optimums for the most part did not again mention this honor to their special nature.

"We failed," declared Pandora dejectedly. "I remember Herodotus said that 'Great deeds are usually wrought at great risks.' In my case, the risk was a painful renewal of the guilt I have so long borne." She paused for reflection. "If any good has come from this fruitless campaign it is the personal bond we have formed. Containing within myself such a load of ancient memories, I should be jaded regarding relationships. Should be, but it seems that I'm not. Never said this before, never. I love you too, Greg."

"That was such a sad ending to a most noble cause," said Aphrodite.

Prometheus nodded in agreement. "I admit to being quite proud of my creation Pandora. She went so far past her limitations. The effort she made was Herculean, and the failure of almost godlike proportions. As the goddess of love, the unlikely romance with her human companion must be pleasing to you."

"To be sure. I would be interested in watching it further develop. Did you create her with the ability to bear children?"

"Why, yes. We endowed her with all human physical attributes and abilities."

"Prometheus, doesn't it seem like Pandora and mankind have been punished enough? After all, you're the one who stole and gave them fire."

"I agree. I have an idea as to how Zeus might be influenced to lighten up on these punishments. Tell me what you think of this." He described his scheme and her smile registered an interest in being a co-conspirator.

Prometheus ended his presentation, "And so, Great Zeus, that describes the drama concerning Pandora and humanity. All of that stemming from your masterful trick of sending the gift box of miseries to the girl created as almost human. It was a most effective punishment for me. Still consumed by guilt, Pandora made a bold effort to reduce these plagues on mankind. Might you consider similarly easing the difficulties of earthlings?"

"Prometheus, you have been forgiven and are again within my good graces. Still, I think the troubles of earthlings may provide a renewed amusement for us in Olympus. I'll start watching them again."

"As you prefer, of course. However, allow me one additional observation regarding the people on Earth and how they envision Your Highness."

"Yes, that would interest me."

Prometheus took a deep breath before boldly proclaiming: *"They don't think of you, or the other gods, or Olympus, at all anymore!"*

"What! How dare they be indifferent? I'll increase their woes! Destroy their planet."

"Wait, please. Hear me out. Over centuries people have replaced their reverence for you, for us, with a belief in their particular religion's singular god. Huge structures, called churches and temples, have been built everywhere for assemblies in which the people reach out to their supposed deities. Most believe that civilization began by their sole god creating the first man and woman."

"How can they believe that? We created their world."

"Might I suggest that their belief in the gods of Olympus might be reestablished by some divine reminder of your preeminence."

Thoughtfully, Zeus murmured, "Hmmm. What might you

propose?"

"Well, Pandora's box of woes demonstrated your omnipotence over their lives. Perhaps some act of benevolence could be the best reminder of the true source of such power. It could show that the mighty Zeus can be merciful when merited, as well as malevolent when flaunted. I believe that humankind will prove just as entertaining to us here in your kingdom if the people were happier with their state."

"Prometheus, you may have convinced me. Anything else?"

"One small request. I created Pandora at your command. I continue to feel compassion for her and am impressed with what she tried to do. I would ask that you grant one single wish of hers, whatever it might be."

"Well, it shouldn't be said that I am primarily a vengeful god."

Pandora and Greg were spending a quiet morning at their home. The baby had not yet awakened. He seemed quite an extraordinary little fellow, though whether these were just parents' typical conceits, or something more, remained to be seen.

The doorbell rang. "I've got a large box for you." The delivery driver set it just inside the door. It was almost too heavy for Greg, who carried it into the living room.

"Did you order something, dear? I didn't," declared Dora.

"Nope," said Greg, "but it is addressed to you. No sender or return address. Wait. There is a message on it. It says, 'The First Gift. Open to dispel all guilt. A Second Gift to Come.'"

With great anticipation they opened the box.

At once there were a flurry of formless spirits that flew from it. They weren't threatening. On the contrary, they were uplifting and altogether wonderful. Dora, using one of her residual skills, was able to identify them. There was *Empathy, Forgiveness, Humor, Tolerance, Trust* and a whole lot more of positive qualities. New gifts to humankind. Clearly these were intended as additions to the *Hope* token concession from the original Pandora's box.

Greg knew from Dora's rapturous expression that this was the most precious gift of all time.

Dora lifted her head toward Olympus with thanks. She gave no thought to what a Second Gift might be. She had everything she wanted.

Many, many years of happiness followed for Greg and Dora and their son Bruce—as close to the name Zeus as possible without burdening the boy with lifelong explanations. Greg became elderly, while Dora did not. They were prepared for this. It didn't reduce their love for one another. Bruce graduated from college and engaged in a humanitarian career with a family of his own.

Greg's time finally expired gently.

Dora was devastated. She had loved this honest, decent man like no other during her long unending life. She was dreading the thought of continuing life without him. After the memorial services she retired to her room to lay on the bed with Greg's picture hugged to her bosom. Unexpectedly, she had an unfamiliar feeling...her life was peacefully draining away. She was losing her immortality. No life was desired without Greg.

The granting of a human death was her Second Gift.

About the author:

John Baldwin has finally acknowledged that he is retired. He has settled in for a comfortable life to best enjoy his wife, daughters, and grandchildren. For so long he operated as an entrepreneur and lawyer. Thereafter, trying his hand at writing, he discovered similarities in the experiences—stimulation in the creativity side and disappointment if the efforts proved unsuccessful. Now instead of presenting the facts of a case, or describing a business opportunity, he aspires to entertain readers. A particular challenge has been to overcome the writing habits that required strict structure and formality for natural and imaginative ways of expression. During this short later career, he has been pleased to have his stories accepted by *Writer's Egg Magazine*, *Two Sisters Publishing* and *U-Rights Magazine*.

WHAT MEN DO
©2021 by Virginia Ewing

Rooster Wilson crept down a narrow hallway sliced with light. He'd slept hard and didn't remember much about the car ride from San Antonio or the arrival in Brownsville. The air in the trailer was heavy with the smell of bacon. He burst into the tiny kitchen. "Boo!"

His father glared. "Jesus H!"

Grampa Frank grabbed him under the arms.

Rooster squirmed. "Let me go!" He escaped and scuttled down the hall to the bathroom as Grampa Frank said, "Good thing the handsome gene skips a generation."

Rooster didn't wait for Doc's reply. He used the bathroom, washed his hands, then stood in the tub to look out the window. He could see across an alley to more trailers and people outside in shorts.

He returned to find his father and Grampa Frank headed out back with bottles of beer. Rooster raised an eyebrow like he imagined his mother would do.

"Don't give me that look," Doc said. "We're on vacation."

Rooster opened the refrigerator. "Can I have a pop then?"

Doc let the screen door slam. "I guess."

Rooster took his breakfast out to the picnic table. Doc and Grampa Frank sat in folding chairs; legs outstretched. His grandfather was gray-haired and tanned, not quite as tall as Doc, but his arm muscles bulged from working on the Indiana farm all spring, summer, and fall.

"Hey, big guy!" Frank called. "Get us a couple more beers."

Rooster sat on the bench. "You promised we'd go fishing," he said.

His grandfather smacked his head. "Right you are. As it happens, I've got everything ready to go. Soon as you've eaten, we'll head out."

Rooster swigged pop too fast, and coughed.

Frank laughed at him. "Slow down! Take us awhile to get the gear together, anyhow. Doc, you bring a pole for the kid?"

Doc lumbered from his chair. "Might be something in the bottom of my suitcase."

Rooster followed with his plate and flopped on the sofa where his father had slept. Plaid upholstery peeped beneath rumpled sheets. Doc pulled a plastic package from under his folded clothes: a child's fishing set, complete with a reel, bobbers, and hooks. "How bout that?"

The thing was flimsy and ridiculous; the old one Rooster used of Tommy's when they went down to the creek was better. He put the set down without opening it and finished his breakfast, sulking while Grampa Frank carted in folding chairs from the yard. Two fully-rigged poles jutted from under one arm. He nudged Rooster's foot with his boot. "I'll get you a real one next time. You'll be big enough to handle it by then."

Doc snorted, picking up the Coleman cooler and heading for the front door.

Rooster carried the plastic toy outside, wondering what the big joke was. He was big enough to handle a real rig, no problem. He lay the set beside the long poles poking out the rear window of the station wagon and climbed in beside the cooler, lifting the lid. Ice bristled with beer and pop. On the floor, a tub with holes punched in the lid squiggled with live minnows.

Frank drove through town then down a sand-swept highway to the coast. Palm trees and clumps of grass waved in the hot breeze. He pulled into a parking area. "The Gulf of Mexico, gentlemen."

Water loomed forever, merging with sky. Gentle waves broke on sand. Deserted beach stretched left and right. "I thought I'd be able to see Mexico from here," Rooster said.

Frank rolled up his window. "Don't you worry, we're going there tomorrow."

They all piled out, Doc grumbling, "I thought we weren't taking the kid."

Frank dragged the long poles out the back window. "You'll get over it."

Rooster dashed down to the water. His grandfather would see to it he wasn't left out of anything. Sand scrunched under his sneakers. He felt like he could run right up into the sky. He flapped his arms, scattering a flock of seagulls. By the time he panted back to the men, they'd set their lines and propped poles in the sand tubes. They'd opened beers and sat watching for a bite.

Rooster put the two halves of his kiddie pole together and tied on a bobber and hook. "I bet ocean fish are too big for this thing," he griped.

Frank gave him a pyramid-shaped weight to use instead of the lead teardrops that came in the package. "This'll help. Tie it a foot past the hook." He showed Rooster how to cast far out into the surf. "The fish'll be there, not close in."

Rooster practiced long casts then stuck his fingers into the slimy tub of minnows, caught one, slipped his hook through its lower lip, and spat on it. He cast over and over, growing restless when nothing bit. The men talked politics like they always did. Doc said, "Eisenhower is going to cook the Russians once and for all," and Frank said, "If they don't cook us first." Rooster rolled up his pants legs and waded along the water's edge, toting his gear to where the coastline curved into a shallow cove. He could just see the tops of the men's heads over a low dune. He dug in the sand. Crabby things with armadillo backs burrowed in the holes.

He ran back to get a pop from the cooler, guzzled it, burped, then scooped minnows from the tub into a rusty bean can he found, and returned to his outpost. He waded into undulating water, casting deep into dark, green places. His stomach rumbled. He had to get a fish, or starve. Something pulled, bending his pole. Line sizzled off the reel. Rooster crouched, yanking to set the hook, walking backwards out of the water, winding the reel until a silver fish with black spots flopped on the bank. It was as long as his arm from elbow to fingertips. "Dad!" He stepped on the line to keep the fish from slipping away. "Dad! Grampa!"

The men waved over the dune, but stayed put. Rooster fumbled for his pocket knife. The set hadn't come with a stringer. Of course. He cut the line, threaded it through one sharp red gill, and tied the fish to his ankle, leaving it to flop in the water. That's what the boys in *The Swiss Family Robinson* would do. He tied the hook and weight back on, using a strong square knot. The speckled fish pulled at his leg. After about thirty minutes he caught two more of the same kind, not as big as the first, but sizable. He gathered the strings together, cut them from his ankle, and walked back to the men, fish held like a prize.

"Son of a bitch!" Doc said.

Rooster eyed the empty bucket between the men.

Frank untangled the lines from Rooster's fingers. "You out-fished us, kid."

Rooster darted a glance at his father but Doc was busy putting his gear away.

Back at the trailer, Frank covered the picnic table with newspaper and lay the three fish on it. "You got my old knife, Doc?" He opened his hand behind his back.

"Forget it," Doc said.

Rooster offered his Scout knife. "You can use mine."

Grampa Frank sneered. "That's as much a toy as that sissy fishing pole your daddy gave you." He captured Doc's wrist, using his free hand to retrieve the pearl-handled pocket knife that Rooster's father always carried. "This was mine before it was yours, thank you very much. What the hell do you think the fillet blade is for."

"Goddammit, Pops." Doc stalked off to the trailer.

Rooster had never heard so much cussing. "I didn't know that was yours, Grampa." The knife was three times the size of his

Scout blade. "Can I see it?"

"Just watch. See this skinny blade?" Frank inserted the tapered point and slit the fish from head to tail, sliding entrails onto the newspaper.

The heart still beat in gleaming innards. Rooster's grandfather scooped it out with the knife tip. "Take it," he said.

The red berry throbbed in Rooster's palm. With each pulse he seemed to see the flap of a tail-fin, a thrust through seaweed. Rooster touched the heart with his fingertip, expecting it to jump. It was more firm than he expected. The tiny muscle contracted twice more then stopped. Rooster rolled it over, flashing on the freezer behind his father's veterinary clinic back home where dead cats and dogs were kept until incinerated. How could a thing alive cease to be?

The next day Frank hurried them through a breakfast of cold cereal. "Mexico waits, men."

Outside was hot as an oven. Dirt puffed in little clouds as they walked to the station wagon.

After driving for some time, they came to a line of cars waiting to cross the Rio Grande. Grampa Frank explained that the two officials in front of a small building would check them through the border. "The bridge is new," he said.

Rooster hung out the window, gazing up at crisscrossed steel girders, the towering beams making him feel somehow powerful, but the river wasn't as big as he thought it would be.

At their turn, one officer took Frank's license while another walked slowly past, peering in the car windows. Their toll was collected and they were waved through.

Beyond the gate, jalopies merged with donkeys carrying baskets of fruits and vegetables. Dogs nosed around dilapidated buildings. The people were short and dark-skinned, and the air was awash in the smell of dog shit and ripe fruit. Rooster's head swiveled from one side to the other; Mexico was even more different from Indiana than Texas.

Frank parked in the shade of a willow tree. "We'll walk to the market," he said. "Roll up your windows and lock the doors."

The Matamoros Market was a confetti of colors, broken only by the dusty white of canvas awnings. Music seeped through the noisy crowd. A double-steepled church towered on the far side. "Stick close," Frank said.

Live chickens cackled in crates. Tortillas sizzled on hot stones. Embroidered blouses swung over tables of silver jewelry. A group of men strummed guitars, swaying under wide sombreros. Coins shone on the tattered velvet of their cases. Tourists in beige pants shouldered straw totes. A wizened man crouched in the crook of two stalls, a rack of colorful spools propped beside him. It took Rooster a moment to realize that the man had no arms. He tugged his father's shirt.

"Beggar," Doc said, walking on.

"But Dad, he's making something." The man's toes were up near his face, wound about with threads that spun from the rack.

"Let the boy look," Frank said.

The armless man's face crinkled. He had only three teeth. He was weaving a tiny sombrero of red, yellow, brown, and turquoise, toes furiously twisting the threads. He finished, cut the strands with his teeth, then handed the tiny thing to Rooster with his strangely curved feet.

Rooster ran his fingers over the hat's tight weave. "Can I buy this for Mom?"

Frank knelt in front of the armless man. "*Cuánto?*"

The hat-maker held up four toes, tucking the big one like a thumb. "*Quatro pesos.*"

"Too much," Frank said. "*Cinco centavos.*"

The man's smile faded. "*Dos Pesos.*"

"*Uno, o nada.*" Grampa Frank gave Rooster a coin. "Pay him."

Rooster placed the money in the palm of a foot, staring as long toes curled, one knee bending to tuck the coin into a pouch.

"*Gracias,*" Rooster said, like his mother had taught him. As they walked away, he asked his grandfather, "How much was that?"

"Fifty cents," Frank told him. "Their money's worth half ours."

Rooster studied the sombrero. It didn't seem like much for something made with toes.

At the next stall, Doc bought a silver necklace for Rooster's mother and a bracelet with ballerina charms for his sister. Then they sat at a taco stand, and Rooster got another pop. Frank ordered "*Dos cervezas.*" From his perch, Rooster spotted a row of curved blades hanging on a line, rattling together like chimes.

"Machetes," Frank said. "Go on, check 'em out."

The noise of the market seemed to grow louder as Rooster pushed through the crowd. Hands brushed against him, but his pockets were already empty. He glanced back to see if Doc was watching. His grandfather shooed him with the back of his hand. At the stall, a skinny man mouthed a cigar behind a table of daggers. He narrowed his eyes and said, "*Qué pasa?*" Overhead, the machetes clanged.

Rooster said, "Just looking." He gazed at the array of knives. The ancient-looking machetes were too big, so he turned to the daggers beneath them, lingering over one with a wavy, silver hilt.

Grampa Frank came and looked over his shoulder. "That's a beauty."

"I don't have any money," Rooster said. "I should've brought my coffee-can bank."

Frank dragged him aside. "Kid, first of all, you need a better bank. Here. Ten pesos." He gave Rooster two crumpled bills. "Keep hold of them until you're ready to pay. You saw how I dickered the price with the hat maker."

Rooster clutched the colorful bills and went back to studying the daggers. He picked up the wavy handled one. "How much?"

"One hundred pesos," the man said, his "R" rolling like grapes.

Rooster's heart sank. The others would be even more expensive. He turned to go.

"*Un minuto,*" the man said, hefting a carton from under the table, the narrow point of his face gone wide and smiling. He shuffled in a jumble of scabbards, and un-sheathed a blade with a bone handle and brass fittings. "How bout dees one?"

Rooster took the dagger. It was etched with swirls and flowers, and very light. The brass fittings jiggled, but maybe they were supposed to. "I only have ten pesos," he said.

The man clapped. "*Perfecto!*"

Rooster gave him the crumpled bills, then tried to roll the R in "*Grazias*" before carrying his prize back through the crowd.

A forest of bottles littered the counter beside Doc and Frank.

"Cheap," Doc said when Rooster showed the dagger.

His grandfather said, "Doc doesn't know squat. Nice work, kid."

Rooster glanced sideways. He suspected his father was right, but he still liked the fancy knife. "You getting anything, Dad?"

"I might be able to think of something later," Doc said. "If certain promises are kept."

"What promises?" Rooster said.

"Everything shuts down at this time of day," Frank said. "We'll siesta, then go someplace special for dinner."

"Ohhhh," Rooster nodded. Doc liked going out for Mexican food back in Indiana.

They wandered past the double-steepled cathedral where scarves draped the heads of women who labored across a cobblestone courtyard on their knees, praying aloud, lace fluttering. It was late afternoon. A sleepy buzz filled the air. Men snoozed on porches of weatherworn bungalows and small children played outside in their underwear.

"Do men ever pray like that?" Rooster asked.

Frank laughed. "Nah. The women do it for them."

When they got to the car, Frank moved it farther into the shade of the willow until branches draped across the roof. They opened the windows and went to sleep in the rustling breeze.

Rooster woke when the car started moving, sitting up, peering around. Trucks, bicycles, and women with bundles moved away from the market now. Hot air flowed across his face. Doc and

Frank smoked as they drove toward a blood red sunset.

It was full dusk when they arrived at a cantina in the desert. Lanterns hung in low trees; torches flamed around a patio. One whole wall opened to the night, and couples occupied candlelit tables both inside and out of the building. Women in ruffled skirts danced between them.

Doc chuckled as they climbed from the car. "Leave it to my pops to know where the action is."

"I have taco sauce on my shirt," Rooster said.

Frank swiped at Rooster's front. "You look fine."

Doc ran a comb through his hair, smoothing with his other hand. "Let's go."

After they were seated inside, a waitress with a flower in her black hair approached. "Margaritas?"

Grampa Frank held up fingers. "*Trés. Uno no tequila.*" He ordered more things in a flood of Spanish. Rooster had no idea what they'd get to eat.

The waitress winked at him when she returned, and her arm brushed his shoulder as she placed a salt-rimmed drink before him. It had a tiny umbrella that opened and closed. Doc's and Grampa Frank's didn't. The men also got small tumblers and an amber-filled bottle that Doc lifted to the light, tapping the glass at something that looked like a maggot.

"What is that?" Rooster said.

"Worms for the worm," Frank said, and he and Doc chuckled.

Rooster stashed the little umbrella away for Evie. He tasted his drink through salt, the green liquid sweet with an edge of something that burned, then finished it fast, like a pop. The men tossed back tumblers of amber liquid and refilled them from the bottle.

Three more margaritas came with dinner. Rooster smiled into the woman's eyes, expert now with the long-stemmed glass. The room glowed. "*Muy atractivo!*" she said, taking his hand.

Frank said something in Spanish. The woman laughed and touched Rooster's cheek. "*Él es dulce.*" She swished her skirt walking away.

"What'd she say?" Rooster mumbled. His tongue had gone numb.

Frank tasted Rooster's almost-finished drink. "Spiked. First one probably was, too."

"Lord, Rooster," Doc said. "Don't tell your mother."

A stupid grin melted across Rooster's face. His stomach was warm and the room spun.

Frank said, "Eat up, kid, before you get sick."

Rooster scraped rice and beans. He'd caught three fish, seen a man with no arms make a hat, bargained at a knife stall, and now he'd had booze. His friend Tommy wouldn't believe it. A man strolled over with a guitar, followed by the waitress who now had wooden clappers on her fingers. Doc slipped pesos into the ruffled pocket of her skirt as she turned, one arm up, waggling her hips. Rooster's stomach lurched when his grandfather patted her bottom. "Grampa," he hissed.

Frank ignored him. The woman bent so that her breasts spilled from the top of her dress. Doc got up to dance with her.

Rooster cast his eyes down. Thick callouses overlapped the heel of the woman's high-heeled sandals. She was missing a toe. But when he looked back up, she smiled at him as before, her face tender. The colors in the smoky room churned. He put his head on the cool table.

Frank pulled him to his feet. "C'mon. Outside with you."

Stars seemed to rise from the torches on the patio, surging in vast swaths across the sky. Frank lit a cigarette and leaned on a post. Rooster gulped air. He kept seeing his father's big hands, low on the woman's waist. "I think we should get Dad and leave."

His grandfather blew smoke in his face. "Don't think so much."

Rooster had never seen his parents dance. His mother often didn't feel well. The starlit sky arched over the raucous Cantina. He'd liked the way the alcohol buzzed in his veins, but now he felt sick. His grandfather was drunk, and his father probably was too.

"Why'd he go off with that woman?"

Frank squeezed his shoulder. "Nothing to worry about."

Rooster narrowed his eyes. "Did you ever bring Gramma here?"

Grampa Frank snorted. "Lord, no. She was tough, though, your grandmother. Good as a man on the farm." He chuckled softly. "But her biscuits were soft as cotton. I do miss her."

Rooster had been told that his grandmother doted on him when he was born. In pictures she was tall and raw-faced, not fine-featured like his mother.

After Frank's fourth cigarette, they went back inside. Doc was coming down a staircase from a balcony over the dance floor, running fingers through his hair. Rooster scanned the high, curtained alcoves. The woman Doc had danced with, and who had been so kind to Rooster, was nowhere to be seen.

His father ambled over, wearing a sheepish grin. Heat rushed to Rooster's face. He clenched his fists. "You think I don't know what's going on?"

Doc adjusted his belt. "Not if you haven't been upstairs you don't."

Blood pounded behind Rooster's eyes. Whatever it was, his mother wouldn't like it. Frank hooted. Rooster threw himself at his grandfather, twisting away from his big hands, hitting at the muscled wall of gut until Doc locked him in a chest hold from behind.

The room had turned red. Rooster hollered, "You goddamn assholes." Laughter rattled over the music as Doc carried him out of the Cantina and set him down beside Frank's station wagon, then stooped over, panting. Rooster's stomach twisted. He fell to his knees by the back tire, swallowing and swallowing to keep from throwing up, aware of his grandfather nearby. "You go on back," he heard Doc tell him. "I'll take care of Rooster."

"I guess I could," Frank said.

As his grandfather sauntered away, Rooster sat on the ground, knees pulled to chest, leaning against the car. His father stood like a cut-out against the sky: the Marlboro Man, un-concerned and satisfied.

"Did you hurt her?" Rooster said, not sure why he thought this might be the case.

"That woman?" Doc said. "Lord, no. *She* like to've hurt *me*."

Rooster wiped his face. How could the sky be so brilliant, the breeze so soft, and the cricket's chirring so gentle? Doc squatted to face him, breath tinged with smoke and tequila. He held out a white object. "Seems like a good time to give you this. A real knife, not like that cheap-ass, waste-of-money dagger you bought. I thought you knew how to hang onto a dollar."

The pearl-handled pocket-knife weighed heavy as stone and warm as a living thing in Rooster's hand. He looked into his father's eyes, turning the knife in his palm, wanting to ask about his mother's illness, about the woman in the Cantina, wanting to be told that everything would be all right. For a moment, the two stayed like that, low to the ground. Then Doc stood to light another cigarette. He gazed up at the stars. "You'll understand when you're a man."

The next morning, Rooster lay awake in his bright bedroom in the trailer. Snores came from his grandfather's room and from down the hall where his father slept on the sofa. The pearl-handled knife rested on his suitcase next to the dagger and his scout blade.

He mulled over the events of the day before. It had all been marvelous, even the terrible part. On the drive back to Brownsville, Rooster had curled in the back seat while in front the men talked about women they'd known. Frank had a girlfriend in Brownsville and was dating someone in Nebraska, too. "I have a pretty good time," Frank said, to which Doc replied in a quiet voice, "Myrna was something before all this. It hurts me, what she's going through."

Frank said, "Myrna was a little too highfalutin for my taste, but I wish her no harm. Think the kid'll keep quiet?"

"You can count on it," Doc had said.

There in the back seat, Rooster had known it was true.

He stuffed his head under his pillow, blocking the morning sun blazing into the trailer. He didn't want to think about anything. He wanted to be home with everything the way it had always been.

By four o'clock their bags were by the door, and Rooster sat at the table with a bottle of pop, ignoring his grandfather.

Across from him, Frank yelled, "Doc! We need to hit it if we're gonna make your train."

Rooster pocketed the pearl-handled knife. "I'll be in the car."

Frank followed him, staring through the window after he'd gotten in and closed the door. Rooster glared down at his knees. Everything would've been fine if they hadn't gone to that place. Grampa Frank didn't care how he felt about anything or about his mother. He began to sweat in the hot car and had to roll the window down, accidentally glancing up. Frank's mouth bent in a half smile. "Hey, kid, it's just the way things are with fellows," he said. "We're the Wilson men. Come on kid. Give an old guy a break." He winked.

Rooster closed his fist around the knife in his pocket and the tightness around his eyes let go some. But for the whole visit, his grandfather hasn't asked him one thing about his playing the drums at school, even though he'd told him about it practically first thing.

The train ride north went by faster than the trip down had. Rooster slept, then finished reading his *Hardy Boys* book. When they rolled into the Chicago station, Doc said, "Maybe we'll do this again next year." Rooster thought how much he would like that, and was glad he'd relented and hugged his grandfather goodbye in San Antonio.

His mother and sister waited on the platform. "You're supposed to be taking it easy, Myrna," Doc said. "I was expecting Fred."

"I'm feeling much better," she said. "We missed you. Didn't we, Evie?"

Evie was all got up in a poufy dress. She shrieked when Rooster surprised her with the tiny umbrellas from his margaritas. Once they were all in the car and Doc was focused on driving, Rooster produced the miniature sombrero. He passed it over the seat to his mother, telling her about the man with no arms.

"What a perfect thing," she said. She turned to smile at him in the back seat. "What else did you boys do?"

"Oh, the usual kinds of things." Rooster gazed at smoke-spewing factories out his window. His mother wouldn't understand what it had been like to be just the boys.

She lifted an eyebrow. "Like what?"

"You know. Fishing. Stuff like that," Rooster said. "Things men do."

About the author:

Virginia Ewing Hudson has won the Thomas Wolfe Fiction Prize and been nominated for a Pushcart Prize. Her poems, essays, and fiction can be found in the *Thomas Wolfe Review, Bosque Journal, Wildflower Muse, Verse Virtual,* and other small presses. "What Men Do," which appears in the Scribe's Valley Anthology, is the third published chapter from a novel-in-progress, *Rooster's Jazz.* She has placed in the Faulkner Society's competition for novels, the Rose Post Competition for creative nonfiction, and the Randall Jarrell Poetry Competition. Virginia teaches cello at Meredith College in Raleigh, North Carolina. She has created a personal writing retreat on a remote mesa in New Mexico where she gives al fresco concerts for neighbors in the summertime. She is revising a new novel set in Oklahoma.

Website: virginiaewinghudson.com

MARY AT 85
©2021 by Virginia M. Amis

"It's a bit airsh," she said when I picked her up from the community where she'd lived for ten years. She liked that word, her lips turning upward at the corners when she used it. Colloquial, something her mother said all the time, she'd told me, pleased with her departure from the King's English. I knew she meant the day was chilling her, even though it was July. She'd worn her raincoat, belted tightly at her small waist, and a felted hat pulled tightly to her ears, once brilliant red, now faded, a muted band around the crown with sprig of silk Edelweiss tucked into it.

I led her away from the sprawling, whitewashed, non-descript buildings that now held her daily life. She held onto my arm, walking a little slower than the last time, moving her feet carefully. She needn't have been concerned. All the paths were straight and level. Nothing disrupted the order of the place. Empty benches, placed precisely at regulated intervals along the sidewalks, watched over the grounds like the guards at Buckingham Palace. No whimsical colors or fancy designs decorating them. No individuality, content in their sameness.

I'd met Mary when she lived in her small brick house across the street from mine. We'd nodded and chatted a few times a week back then, polite neighbors, both busy with our husbands. Then, her Bill died, beloved Bill. The man with whom she'd traveled the world, who lit the lamps in her blue eyes every time she looked at him. I'd seen her adore him, even from a neighborly distance. The man of her adventures.

The ambulance came one morning and that was that.

Afterwards, I watched more closely. I saw Mary drive herself to the grocery store and to her doctor appointments. She tended her small garden and went to church on Sundays. Sometimes she had a visitor, but not often.

The arguments in my house, quiet deep disagreements, shook me to the core. Why was he staying out later in the evenings? Where was he going on Saturdays when we should have been together?

Sitting on the front step, fuming from our latest disagreeable conversation, I watched Mary don her garden gloves and look around for her hand spade. Without planning to, I walked across the street and helped her plant the tray of purple, yellow and orange pansies she'd bought that morning. She made sure not to let me organize them in rows or patterns.

"They look better when they are spread in no particular way," she'd told me as though I'd challenge her. I remember looking back at my own garden and seeing my pansies, all purple, in straight rows.

"I like a flurry of color, like you see in an English garden. All sorts of flowers in all colors, growing together. Its fine, too, if you plant the same flowers together, so long as they are planted to look like they just sprung up in your garden naturally. Mix up the colors! Have an adventure."

I could not help but smile.

"Bill and I used to seek out all the gardens we could find when we traveled. Have you ever seen the fields of roses in Regent's Park? Acres of them, every color of the rainbow." Her eyes looked into the distance as she pictured them.

I hadn't been to England. It was not looking like I'd be traveling anywhere but to find my own apartment anytime soon. Mary noticed my melancholy.

"You don't have to purchase a plane ticket to go anywhere," she said, pointing to her temple. "I live in my dreams most days now. Bill gave me that gift. He was a dreamer, you know."

I began visiting her for longer stretches, having lunch, taking her extra cookies I'd baked. She never returned the cookie dish empty.

We kept in touch, even after I moved to my little drab apartment five miles away. As her eyesight dimmed, I insisted she sell her car and let me drive her places. Finally, the house became too much for her to handle.

"Watch your step. The path's a bit uneven here."

Mary seemed not to hear me. "I like the zinnias best this time of year. But nasturtiums are fine, too. My mother used to call them 'nasties.' Made us kids laugh."

"Well then," I said as I held firmly on to her arm. "Let's go down the path toward the zinnias. You said its best to plant the dwarf ones with the tall variety. Let's see what the gardeners have for us."

I took her a few more steps, seeing only the straggling pale remnants of early spring pansies hanging on in a futile attempt to extend their lives beyond what nature intended.

"Oh, my gosh! You were right! The shorts and talls look marvelous together. They are a sea of pinks and oranges."

She knew I was lying, but I saw satisfaction cross Mary's face. "So, you were listening. Sometimes I wonder if anyone listens to an old woman anymore."

I blushed. There were times when I did not listen. Like when she started in on the story about the puppy that dug up her mother's chrysanthemum garden, a story I'd heard nearly every week when I gathered her for our walks.

"Guess what's next. Can't see them yet...." It was a game we played.

"Roses! I smell roses. Perfume delight, Peace, Marilyn Monroe..."

"And, Mr. Lincoln," I added. My voice gave her the vision she did not have. She knew there was not a rose anywhere around my apartment complex. Any fragrance she detected lived in her memory.

"Perfume Delight smells the best!" she said. "Heaven cannot

smell any better."

She mentioned heaven a lot more often lately.

We shuffled along as I continued the tour. A car horn blared loudly from the interstate highway a few hundred yards away. We both pretended not to hear it.

"Remember the lilacs blooming earlier this year? They are my favorite."

Mary nodded, knocking her glasses down her nose. I waited while she adjusted them.

"The darker the blooms, the more intense their scent. My father loved lilacs. Every year, they bloomed around his birthday, May first. We kids picked armloads and placed them in anything that would hold water—vases, pitchers, old mayonnaise jars—so he would see them everywhere when he came home from work." She lifted her face to the sun, remembering. "Bill loves them, too."

I looked at her to see if she realized her error. Bill had been gone for thirteen years.

Paths wound around my apartment complex and we shuffled them slowly, pretending they were a grander locale. I only brought her here because it was close by and the short distance did not tax her too much. She looked forward to our visits and sorely needed a change from her sterile daily surroundings. But she tired more quickly these days. We used to go to the parks along the lake, hear the birds calling to each other, have a picnic lunch and admire the bachelor buttons and coreopsis growing together in the wild flower fields. She could no longer see well enough to distinguish more than shapes. Now, her memory and I were her vision.

A few more paces along, she stumbled on a sidewalk crack. I reached to steady her.

"You stepped on an alligator."

She laughed, her voice sounding a little weaker than the last time we walked. "I'm a little tired today. Can we go back to the chateau?"

Inside my small apartment, I lowered her into a familiar easy chair. Her arms reached out on both sides, searching.

"I'll bring it to you," I said, retrieving her white cane from the corner.

I settled on the sofa and reached out my hand to grasp one of hers. "Did you like your garden tour today? The Arboretum is one of my favorites."

"Yes, it was lovely," she replied.

"Where would you like to go next week?"

She thought for a moment, her gnarled hands on her cane. "Regents Park. Bill and I went there on our honeymoon. There is an entire field of nothing but roses. I'd like to see that again."

She'd told me that story a hundred times. "London, then. I'm sure I can arrange it. And the week after?"

She pulled a tissue from her pocket and dabbed her eyes. "Let's not be too ambitious. How about the gardens at Versailles?"

About the author:

Virginia Amis is a lawyer and a writer, who spends her days in the courtroom and her nights and weekends writing. A transplant from Pittsburgh to the Pacific Northwest, she often writes in that setting, bringing nature and characters to life through her stories. She has written two novels and is working on a third. She has published stories in the 2018, 2019 and 2020 issues of *Perspectives Magazine*, 2020 issues of *Reminisce* and *Reminisce Extra*, 2018 and 2019 Scribes Valley Anthologies, *Linden Avenue Literary Journal*, March 2020 issue, and in *101words.com*.

WANDERER
©2021 by Sonia Mehta

Lexi's stomach had been in knots for the better part of an hour. Her knuckles turned white, but she could not let go of the side railing of the ancient ferry carrying her over the Bering Sea. Fog hung like a stifling veil over the boat, swallowing it and muffling the invisible waters. Lexi felt suffocated. *I am only sixteen, I don't want to die here.* The wind whipped her chestnut hair, and she regretted wearing her designer jeans.

"Don't worry," her father reassured, moving closer, "the captain can navigate these waters with his eyes closed. The fog usually clears by midday. You'll warm up once we get to the island. Remember, Unalaska has—"

"Wi-Fi. I know."

Her father lowered his dark blue eyes. Lexi looked at the tall man who had been absent from her life for the last year. She regretted her tone. He had not forced her to spend the summer with him in the least hospitable place on the globe. She missed him and wanted to come.

"Lexi, I haven't seen you since the divorce."

"Whose fault is that? Who made you leave Galveston? You had tenure at A&M Maritime. Why would you give it up and move to the Aleutians? It's not like the Department of Fishes offered you more money."

"Bureau of Fish and Wildlife."

Lexi rolled her eyes. Every conversation they had ended on an unpleasant note.

"If you don't like it, you can go back to Texas," her father offered.

***

At last, the boat docked at Dutch Harbor. The fog had lifted, revealing a fairy-tale picture: moss-carpeted mountains and dozens of American bald eagles perched on the lamp posts against a blue satin sky. Lexi could hardly wait to start taking pictures and posting them for her friends to see.

"Don't get too excited. Bald eagles are as common as pigeons here. In fact, be mindful of where you are at all times. They do attack if you get too close to their nests."

Lexi glared at her father, not bothering to thank him for the unrequested advice. She turned away to take in the view and the scent of the sea. There were half a dozen large crab boats docked at Dutch Harbor. Rows and rows of crab pots, 800-pound wire mesh cages, were stacked at the aft of each one. It was cold and windy, but Lexi was ready to start taking pictures worthy of National Geographic.

Rain drizzled as they walked to their car. "The locals joke: it doesn't rain on the islands, it rains in Russia, and the wind blows it here," her father tried to bring a smile to Lexi's sullen face. She was not amused.

They took the Airport Beach Road that connected the smaller Amaknak Island, where Dutch Harbor was, to Unalaska via a bridge. As the pair drove through the town, Lexi could not tell which century she entered. The structures were small, painted in contrasting colors, and built-in peculiar styles. Her father's house, a plain white bungalow, sat on the side of a hill overlooking the sea. It had three rooms, each slightly smaller than the preceding one, like a toy collapsible telescope laying on its side. The inside of the house was clean and blessedly warm.

Lexi went to her bedroom to unpack while he prepared dinner. Half an hour later Lexi came to the kitchen to help him.

"What exactly do you do in Alaska, Dad?"

"I test the water conditions around the islands, especially the fifty-five uninhabited ones. What really brought me here, other than the events in Texas, was the chance to study kelp."

"You left me to look at seaweed," she mumbled, tugging at her hoop earring.

"Kelp provides shelter and food for countless species that are endangered by climate change. Do they teach you about global warming?"

Lexi sighed, "Of course they do. I know that my generation is doomed. So, we might as well crank up the AC for the short time we have left."

"We're not doomed yet. And kelp could play a role in saving.... Anyways, I won't bore you with all that, Lexi. I'm really glad you're here!"

Dinner, a microwaved can of stew, made her melancholy again. It was such a contrast to the multi-course meals their family used to share. She sat at the table pushing a chunk of meat around her plate.

"Dad, I'm a vegetarian now. All my friends are. You just don't get it. They'll judge me!"

"We have edible seaweed."

"No, thanks, I don't want to deprive the fish and bring down the ecosystem. Need to do my part in saving the earth." Lexi was glad none of her friends would see her eating beef. She was not going to post that picture.

She slept fitfully that night and wondered if she would adapt to the sun staying up past midnight. When she woke up a few hours later, her father had already left for one of the islands. On the kitchen table, a note read, *Lexi, sorry, I didn't think about the fruits and veggies. I will look for some today.* A plate of spam and eggs waited in the microwave. She groaned, but heated her plate and guiltily enjoyed the flavor of the mystery meat.

It was time to explore. Lexi pulled on a duffle coat over her maroon A&M sweatshirt and walked down the wooden plank walkways to town. Dozens of bald eagles perched on the electric towers, staring at her as though keeping her under CCTV surveillance. Within four hours, Lexi had wandered through every aisle of every store that did not sell hardware. This would be a long summer. White fog rolled in, and Lexi felt cold water on her cheeks. Time to head back to the house.

Her father was already home.

"Where are you going tomorrow, Dad?"

"To Tuk Island. Do you want to come?"

"Yes! There's nothing to do here."

The following morning, Lexi and her father climbed into his cuddy boat. It was old and loud but charming. She felt like Snow White entering the dwarfs' floating cottage. Every piece of furniture was a miniature of a real thing. The spell was broken when she spotted his salinometer, hydrometer, and a bin of test tubes in a corner. The scientific equipment was a painful reminder of why her father left her in Texas and moved to this godforsaken place.

"Batten down the hatches," Lexi heard his command.

"Huh?"

"Three sheets to the wind," her father teased.

"What?"

"Don't you know any nautical terms?"

"Yeah, I do. 'Two ships passing—silently—in the night.' Is that nautical enough for you?"

The corners of her father's mouth turned down. Lexi immediately regretted her stinging retort. She knew that in his awkward way he was trying to rebuild the ties frayed by more than distance.

"Dad, I do know the nautical terms for a pirate's favorite letter."

"Rrrr?"

"No, Dad, de C."

They both laughed as only father and daughter could.

After several hours of island hopping, the boat arrived at Tuk Island.

"So, there is no one on this island?"

"No one but us, Lexi. It's owned by the Department of Defense for reasons even they probably forgot. They own several islands around here. You'll see some 'No Trespassing' signs. But we're okay. No one's here to find us."

"Can I go ashore? Unless there are bears."

"No bears, just a lot of birds. You can take the dinghy. Just don't go too far from the shore. Make sure you can see my boat. Take the walkie-talkie too. There's no service out here. I'll be doing water testing for a couple of hours so don't stay out too long."

Lexi paddled the short distance to shore and secured the boat's rope to a rock. Turning around, she saw her father's steady gaze, waved, and started walking along a narrow pebble beach. Beyond a raised dune of tall grass were the first trees, evergreens, that were almost her height, barely over five feet. The branches were all to one side, opposite to the coastal winds. They resembled green-haired girls with their long manes blown aside from a hairdryer.

Further ahead a stream emptied its crystal water into the sea. Short green grass and moss carpeted the ground leading up the mountain. *I'll climb to the water source*, Lexi mused, *like an African explorer discovering the Nile's origin.* She hiked up; her thoughts were purified by the gurgling water. *Perhaps Dad hadn't abandoned our family. Maybe he was pulled here by a desire to find solace that he'd never known. I should stop blaming him for being a human with a human weakness.*

The trail took a sudden turn, and Lexi lost her train of thought. She gazed in awe at a narrow, twenty-foot waterfall. *These islands are a part of some enchanted world.* A small pond shimmered at the base of the fall, its banks covered with verdant ferns. Tiny, luminescent red and green fish darted between reflected leaves, like blinking lights on a Christmas tree. Lexi whipped out her phone and took several pictures. Tucking it safely away, she noticed shiny red berries and remembered that they were called wild salmonberries. She pulled one from a thicket and squeezed a spray of red juice. She held it to her nose, certain it was edible.

On her right was a dry creek bed, lined with smooth stones.

Walking down this side of the mountain along the stone creek was easier. Her route became obstructed by a large boulder. She could scale it. She had always been athletic and nimble from years of gymnastics. Her toe found a crevice, as did her fingers. Heaving herself up, she almost reached the top when she came face to face with a yellow-eyed white head with a huge hooked beak. The bald eagle screeched and raised its talons to strike. Lexi instinctively pushed away and rolled down the mountainside. Her arms flailed, searching for something, anything, to break her fall. Feeling a branch, she grabbed it with both hands. The sapling was weak. She looked for something sturdier and spotted a conifer tree to her right. She had no choice. She swung her legs. The sapling broke, but her right hand reached and found the trunk of the tree. *Thank you, high school PhysEd.* With one last heave, she pulled herself up and sat atop the narrow ledge.

From her perch, she could see her father's boat bobbing in the distant cove. *Great view*, she thought, tucking away a strand of curly hair into her ponytail. *All I had to do was fall off a mountain to see it.* Next to her was another patch of wild salmonberries. This time she did not hesitate, grabbed a handful, and dropped the floral-scented berries on her tongue.

Now, I need to head back. Discovering the Nile's source will have to wait. As she turned to leave, Lexi noticed a baseball-size hole in the side of the mountain wall. She edged closer, and a space behind it revealed itself. Lexi turned on the flashlight function on her iPhone and peered into the darkness. There was a cave behind the rubble of stones. Her flashlight scanned the back wall and bounced off a luminescent drawing: a series of intersecting circles in a crisscross pattern. She hesitated to explore further. Then an object near the cave's entrance came into view. Reaching in, Lexi withdrew a golf ball-size red stone set in silvery metal. Curved lines were engraved in the broach that felt like ice in Lexi's hand. The object sparkled in the sun as if it had been waiting for this moment to shine. She pocketed the jewel.

The discovery vanquished any hesitation of further exploration.

Lexi pulled out more stones and crawled through the enlarged opening. The cave was about ten feet long and not tall enough for her to stand straight. She stooped in order to reach the back wall. Kneeling in front of the drawing, Lexi pondered its meanings. A star chart? It looked familiar but not quite. Was it the Big Dipper? On her left, a narrow tunnel led to a chamber. In the middle of the cavern stood an object. A stalagmite? A white glow radiated from above. Lexi crawled the short distance towards the light column. She looked up and pointed her light at a...man. He sat cross-legged, facing another star chart. Lexi arched up from the sight of the tall figure with luminescent white hair. Her head hit the ceiling of the cave. The man remained motionless. She scampered backwards through the tunnel, bolted out of the cave, and propelled herself down the mountain.

Please, be there, Dad!

She untied her dinghy, jumped in, and paddled furiously towards the boat. *Who was that?* She slowed down and stopped rowing, recollecting the events in the cave. A clear vision of the star chart and the man came to her mind. He was enormous with long, white hair and taut, unmarked skin. He sat cross-legged, his head touching the top of the cave, staring at the chart.

Her eyes widened at the realization. She had found a mummy.

"You weren't gone long, Lexi. See anything interesting?" her father's cheerful voice broke through her thoughts.

She looked up at him on the deck. She would tell him everything, but not until she understood what she had found.

"Just some wild berries." Lexi felt guilty. She did not know why, but she felt the need to protect the mummy.

"Are you going to come with me tomorrow?" her father asked as they docked their boat at the harbor several hours later.

"I don't think so. I want to explore the town a bit more. There is the Museum of the Aleutians here. I want to learn about this place."

"Good idea! I spent a year here but don't know much about the history of this place. Let me know what you learn. There is also a Russian church and cemetery in town. We could explore it together one day."

Lexi spent several days at the museum and online learning about the Aleuts. They were a minority on their own land, less than ten thousand still living on the islands. Most had died of European diseases. Others had been massacred by Russian seal-fur trappers.

"Learned anything, Lexi?" her father asked one evening.

"Yeah, a Russian officer had lined up ten natives, tied together by a rope, and fired a cannon at one end to see how many bodies the shot would penetrate."

"Are you serious?" disbelief showed on his face.

"Yes, six."

That night Lexi stood at the porch and stared at the billions of stars littering the sky. The island was silent except for the distant sea. She had not truly seen the night sky until she arrived in Unalaska. The solitude and darkness were absolute. Lexi thought about the Big Dipper in the cave. The constellation in the sky was similar to the cave's chart but something was off. She felt the cold garnet jewel in her pocket. The meaning of its curved engravings was no clearer. Nothing Lexi had learned made sense. Mummified Unangan remains had been found over the years. But the 8000-year-old Native Americans were always buried in shallow graves close to a village. Her wanderer—that's what she called him—bore no resemblance to the pictures and descriptions she had seen. His enormous height and lack of tattoos or piercings were at odds with native culture.

The jewel was nothing like the stone, shell, or bone adornments typical of the Aleutians. The carvings on the stone and the star chart on the cave's wall were a riddle. Lexi took the jewel from her pocket and held it against the black sky. She turned it upside down. That was not it. She turned it around. The carvings lined up with the seven stars of the Big Dipper. Then she understood. The constellation on the wall was a rendering from the other side of the galaxy. Lexi held the unusual stone against the sky again. The jewel became warm in her hand and turned translucent. She looked through it and saw another star, right in the middle of the Big Dipper's cup. Lexi looked at the sky with her naked eye; the star was not there. It was visible only when she looked through the wanderer's jewel.

Who were you? A wanderer from a faraway planet? Were you wishing you could go back home on your last day on Earth?

She listened to the sounds of the frigid night. Perhaps her wanderer had something in common with her father. Lexi gazed up again. *I don't know who you were. But I have no right to disturb your resting place.* She shivered and went inside for the night. Her father sat by the blazing fire, reading.

"Dad, can we go to Tuk island tomorrow? I want to show you something."

"Sure thing, Lexi. What's there?"

"It's better if you see it."

They left early and had breakfast of coffee and bagels on the boat.

"Dad, you have to promise not to tell anyone about what I'll show you. I want to protect...it."

"Very mysterious, Lexi. But okay, I promise. Unless someone is in danger," he corrected himself.

When they got to the island, Lexi took her father to the cave. "Dad, I may not understand your reasons for coming here. But I know you had them. Everyone has the right to wander the universe and to find a peaceful place."

She did not give him a chance to reply. "Ready?" Lexi pointed to the entrance.

About the author:

Sonia Mehta is an emerging writer living in Ohio. Her stories have been published in *Apprentice Writer* (Susquehanna University), the *Secret Attic, Blue Marble Review, Ice Lolly Review,* and *Cathartic Literary* magazines. She has attended the Iowa Writers' Workshop. She loves writing because it gives her a chance to pour her quirky ideas onto paper without fear of ridicule. That comes later.

www.ingramcontent.com/pod-product-compliance
Lightning Source LLC
Chambersburg PA
CBHW071400170626
46811CB00003B/1195